SHE'S A REBEL

SHE'S A REBEL

Hollywood Writers' Room Book Three

JAEL TEMPTS

ALSO BY JAEL TEMPTS

Hollywood Writers' Room

She's a Rainbow

She's Got a Way

First Printing 2021

ISBN: 978-1-955264-01-3

E-ISBN: 978-1-955264-00-6

Written by Jael Tempts

Editing by Beth Hale, Magnolia Author Services

Cover Art by 100covers.com

❀ Created with Vellum

PART ONE

"Love Her Madly"

Chapter One

JARROD (OVER FOUR YEARS AGO)

I was always the last passenger to board a plane. This was by design. It was the best way to avoid gawkers with their ever present cell phone cameras. Usually, I would relax in the VIP lounge until an attendant came to escort me to the gate.

An attendant escorted me this time, but we were in one of those stupid cars equipped with a bicycle bell of all things, as if that was could persuade anyone to move. He rang the bell. Some people looked. Others kept walking, staring at their phones, oblivious. Of those who looked, a good portion did double takes and pulled out their phones, this time pointed at me.

"Hey, Jarrod Colosi!"

Yes, that was my name. I plastered on a fake smile and gave a slight nod.

"Do the Chuckles laugh!" someone called.

I ignored that one. I'd played a maniacal zombie clown almost fifteen years ago. It had become a cult classic, but I wouldn't call it a career high point. The bell was doing even less to clear our path now.

"Maybe I'd do better on foot?" I suggested.

The attendant shook his head. "No, sir. They want me to take you to the gate."

My flight out of Heathrow had been delayed, and now the airline was holding this flight for me. I didn't want to push the boundaries of their hospitality. It wouldn't take much to let the plane go without me aboard. I tried pulling my hat down so I would be less recognizable. That helped about as much as the stupid bell.

"Everyone, please, make a path for the cart!" A woman's commanding voice rang out over the din. "Pick a side and move to it. Your cooperation is most appreciated. That's right, just like when you're down the shore. 'Watch the tram car, please.'" She said the last in a nasal, mechanical voice that garnered more than a few laughs. The crowd parted. She walked briskly ahead of us the rest of the way to the gate.

"Ree-ree, you're a lifesaver," my driver said. I jumped out the moment we rolled to a stop and got my bag.

"You are," I agreed, and added to the attendant, "Thanks for the ride."

Ree-ree, whose real name was ReAnne according to her nametag, strode purposely to the desk by the gate. "We can't hold an entire flight because he's afraid to raise his voice," she confided as she scanned my ticket. "Enjoy your flight, Mr. Colosi."

"Thank you, Ree-ree." I gave her my most charming smile.

She grinned. "Off with you. There's no time."

I hurried down the jetway to where a flight attendant waited at the door. "Welcome aboard, Mr. Colosi," he said.

"Sorry I'm late."

"No problem, sir. You're just here. Second row on the right. I'll stow your bag."

It was the only empty seat in the first class cabin. Usually,

I had my assistant buy the seat next to me too. That hadn't been possible this time. I took my messenger bag with me and stepped over to my seat.

"There's just time for a drink, sir. Can I get you something?"

"Scotch, neat."

"Miss? Would you like something?"

"Ginger ale, please," the woman in the seat next to mine said.

He was back a moment later with our drinks. My seatmate glanced at me and gave me a tight smile that didn't rise above her cheekbones. She was Latina and pretty. Her dark hair was pulled back in a braid, but a few curls had escaped. I'd seen the recognition on her face when I boarded, but she didn't say anything, which was a pleasant change.

The attendant collected our empty cups before going through the safety protocols. I noticed my seatmate listening carefully. Tension rolled off her in waves. Her fingers beat out a steady, silent staccato on her denim clad thighs. She checked the seat pocket for an air sickness bag and glanced over at mine, too. *Great, a nervous flyer.* That could explain why she was so quiet. I could have turned on the charm and gotten her to relax. Any other day, I would have, but I'd already spent most of my day traveling and didn't feel like making small talk for the next six hours. I closed my eyes and waited for takeoff.

When I opened them again, we were in the air. My seatmate had relaxed. She wore headphones connected to an MP3 player on her lap and typed furiously on a laptop. I glanced curiously at the screen and saw the familiar formatting of a script. I suppressed a groan. The curse of being a director was that everyone wanted me to read their scripts. Everyone had one, the waiter in the restaurant, the valet parking attendant. One time, a hotel maid even left one on my pillow next to the mint. I put earbuds in my ears. The woman next to me didn't even glance my way. I pulled the script for my current project out of my bag and started making notes. Maybe if she saw I was already working on something, she'd leave me alone.

The flight attendants offered dinner. I ate automatically and washed it down with more scotch, then got another refill before losing myself in my work again. As we flew over the Rockies, my seatmate's fingers finally slowed and stopped, hovering over the keyboard. She seemed to come back to herself and slowly remember where she was. She caught me looking at her and smiled. "What a coincidence, right? Ending up next to each other on the same flight to L.A. I mean."

"Yeah," I said. And then because I was tired and had been drinking most of the day, I added, "Look, I'm just going to say this and get it out of the way. I'm sorry, but I'm not going to read your script, okay?"

She opened her mouth to object.

"I don't want to hear about it, either," I said as gently as I could manage.

Her mouth closed with a click.

This could go one of two ways. Either she would be embarrassed, and we'd spend the rest of the flight in awkward silence, or she would cause a scene.

Her eyes, they were golden brown, I noticed, the color of good whiskey, narrowed. "Oh, really?" she drawled.

And here came the scene. I braced myself and waited for my day to get a lot worse.

"I hate to break it to you, Mr. Jarrod Colosi." The way she pronounced my name, every syllable stabbed like sleet in the winter. "But you already *are* reading my script."

Okay, that wasn't what I expected.

"Check the name on the cover. Go ahead, I'll wait." She typed quickly on her keyboard while I flipped the pages. "See that name? Samantha Augustine?" She turned her laptop so I could see the screen.

She'd pulled up a cover of one of the top entertainment magazines. The headline proclaimed, "It's Samantha Augustine's world and we're happy to live in it." And there was my seatmate, but in full makeup. In the picture, her hair was down, falling over her shoulders in a mass of dark curls. I'd noticed she was pretty, but the truth was, she was beautiful. Not in the photo, though that was great, right there in the flesh, her face just a little flushed, her eyes flashing, those wild dark curls that refused to be tamed. She was beautiful, and I'd just acted like an asshole.

"Hello again, Mr. Colosi, I understand we'll be working together." Her eyelashes fluttered over eyes that shot daggers.

"I-I'm sorry," I stammered. "I didn't realize..."

"Didn't realize I was worth a bit of common courtesy?" she finished for me. "I'm obviously not the Hollywood type, so I must want something from you. That's it, isn't it?"

"It's been a long day."

"Oh, boo-freaking-hoo. You spent the day on a plane in first class with flight attendants ready to jump the moment you say 'boo'. I've flown first class from London. It's damn comfortable, and the food is excellent."

I opened my mouth, but she held up her hand. "Don't bother trying to think of another excuse."

She gathered up her things.

"Where are you going?"

"I bet I can find a fangirl back in coach who would just *love* to switch seats with me. I might warn her that one's heroes are best admired from afar." Samantha Augustine snapped her laptop shut and started to stand.

I caught her arm. "Please, don't."

She looked at my hand and back at my face. Her eyebrows rose. I removed my hand. "I'm sorry," I said. "I'm grumpy and rude and... an ass. Don't go." I assumed my best sad face, the one that drove the fangirls wild.

Her face softened the slightest bit. "Fine." She sighed. "Don't give me the big brown eyes. I won't let anyone know you're here." To herself, she muttered, "God, forbid."

"Let me apologize," I said.

She turned to face me again, and I saw that her irritation had not dissipated in the least. "I'm going to listen to some music until we land. At which point, we are going to get off this plane and go our separate ways. And when we see each other at the preproduction meeting in two days, we're going to pretend that we're meeting for the first time. Understand?"

"Look," I said.

"Stop. Talking," she snapped. She turned away without waiting for a response.

I sank back in my seat. Samantha Augustine, author of the script on my lap, scowled at her MP3 player as she turned her music up loud enough that I could hear it escape her headphones.

All her stuff was packed and ready, so when we landed, she was the first person off the plane. I watched as she stormed away from me, not running, but definitely power walking at a speed I couldn't match. *Great job, Colosi,* I thought, *you're off to a wonderful start.*

All I ever got was that false start, because Samantha Augustine backed out of her contract and never joined the production. I tried to contact her through her agent. She was the creator and showrunner on three network shows. I sent flowers to every office she had. Nothing could get her back on the project, and she refused to speak to me.

Chapter Two

SAMI

I strode onto the set of *Death Sucks* with my travel mug of mochaccino in one hand and my new Theo L. designer briefcase in the other. Our dress code on set was pretty casual. I would dress up my jeans and t-shirt with heels and a blazer for table read days, but today I wore a suit. My hair was loose and curly, which was a look I generally saved for events. Hell, this was an event. We were reading the season finale. I had the writer credit for this episode. I was always listed as the show creator and executive producer. This time, though, my name would appear under "directed by" as well. That had never happened before. I'd been assistant director several times, but that was just the learning process. Every part of this finale was mine, and I couldn't be more pleased.

We'd done two read-throughs in the writers' room. Normally, we only did one, but I'd wanted to have every beat perfect before handing it over to the talent. The assistants, interns, and runners all vied for a chance at our read-throughs. It meant limitless candy, a nice lunch and a chance to make an impression. Desi had connections all over Hollywood and was more than happy to put in a good word. Kassi wasn't a networker. She was more comfortable in the literary field, but she could talk plots and characters for hours with an aspiring writer. And then there was me. Desi had her film scripts, though she'd stepped back from that for a while to work with me, and Kassi had her novels, which she cranked out at an alarming rate. I had my television shows, three of them to be precise, and I was working on a fourth. Desi joked that I wanted my own empire. She wasn't wrong. My people, and they were *my* people, often moved up from one set to another. I liked handing out opportunities, and I liked working with artists I could trust. Everyone on a set was an artist. Once you recognized that, it made things a lot easier.

Mickey, my right hand person on every one of my sets, fell into step next to me. "Morning, Sami."

"And a good morning it is," I said, ignoring that they hadn't said the "good" part. "Is everyone here?"

"Pretty much. We have a few minutes. Maybe we could..."

Kassi hurried out of some out of the way spot where she'd been lingering. She never liked to enter the room until we were ready to begin. Arriving early might force her to talk to people.

"Sami, what's going on? Why aren't you answering your phone?" Kassi's frosty blue-green eyes were wide.

"I was getting to that," Mickey said.

"I had the ringer off," I said. I tried to keep it off on the weekends. Anything that happened on a Monday morning could wait until I got to the set. "What's wrong?"

Kassi rubbed her palms on her jeans and looked to Mickey. "Do you know why he's here?"

"Who? What are you talking about?"

Mickey chewed their lip. "The network made a change."

I gave them my full attention. "I'm sorry, what?"

Kassi's mouth fell open. She looked ready to run away. "No one told you," she said. It wasn't a question.

"Told me what?" I waited for Mickey to answer.

"We have a guest director for the finale. The network didn't go looking for one, but he offered, and he's really hot right now. They thought it would be a great promotional opportunity since he just won an Oscar..." Mickey's voice trailed away at the end.

"And this happened when?" I asked, my voice low and dangerous.

"Over the weekend, from what I can tell," Mickey said. "Apparently, he's old friends with the head of the network. Lewis Davies was like a second father back in his television days." They were careful not to say the particular name that would make my head explode. "He wanted to guest direct and the only show left was the finale."

My finale. I thought, but didn't say the words out loud, because as much as I wanted to channel my daughter and throw a tantrum right then, this was my world, and I had to set an example. If I showed disrespect to our "visiting" director, it would filter through to the whole set and the finale would suffer. *It was supposed to be mine.* "I need to duck into my office," I said. "I'll be there in just a few minutes."

"I'm sorry, Sami," Mickey said.

"You're just the messenger," I said and forced a smile. Lewis Davies would pay for that too. I didn't care if he was president of the damn network. Everyone on my set was family, and no one got to make my family uncomfortable.

Mickey seemed happy to escape. Kassi stayed and followed me into my office. "I wish Desi was here," she said softly.

"It's fine," I said. Desi, the third member of our exclusive *tres amigas* club, was in Iceland. Apparently, her boyfriend needed some support. *I need support*, I thought selfishly, but pushed that thought away. Desi would be on the next flight if I called her. Whatever Patrick's problem was, she'd leave him and come running if I asked. *Would she?* some small part of me asked. I pushed that away too. Of course she would.

"Fine?" Kassi asked.

"Fine except for that asshole waltzing in here and taking over *my* finale." I slapped my hand on my desk. Kassi flinched.

"Maybe it's an attempt to get close to you. He tried working with your friends. The next logical step would be to try working with you again."

"Whose side are you on?" I asked, but it wasn't much of an accusation. I knew better.

"Yours," Kassi answered promptly. "Always." She held out a hairband.

I took it without another word. Despite the sheer mass of my hair, weaving it into a braid only took a minute. I wanted to change my clothes, but that would be too pathetically obvious. I'd already been seen by a dozen or so people. A hairstyle was no big deal. I usually wore my hair up and out of the way. Which was worse: being over-dressed when I was supposed to be making my directorial debut or changing into more casual clothes when I publicly discovered I wouldn't be getting that chance after all?

"I could lure him behind the dumpster later, and we could beat him up," Kassi said, breaking into my thoughts. "Though he'd probably enjoy that," she added slowly.

I laughed, mostly because Kassi wanted me to. It wasn't fair. He shouldn't be able to just waltz into my world like he belonged there. I'd had to bargain, persuade and outright manipulate myself into the director's chair for this episode. He got there in the space of one conversation. One. It didn't matter that he was a well-known, Oscar winning director, and I was just the showrunner. I knew my show better than anyone except for the woman standing next to me and the third member of our writers' room, Desi. Had he ever even watched an episode of *Death Sucks*?

"You can do this," Kassi said with absolute confidence. "Come on. Chin up, tits out. We don't play."

"We slay," I answered. This was a role reversal. I was the one who gave the pep talk when Kassi didn't want to go out on stage or enter a room full of people.

"We don't walk," she said.

"We strut."

"Let's go in there and make them want us," she said. "That should be easy, since he already wants you," she added with a sidelong glance.

I frowned, but she offered me a cherry lollipop. She must have gone into the writers' room and gotten it when she spotted him, our guest director, Jarrod Colosi.

*S*ami finally entered the room, and I lost track of my conversation. The kid talking to me had one of those faces that would make him look like a teenager when he was forty. I would have hated him if he hadn't been so damn earnest. Everyone on this set was like that, full of excitement, even if all they were doing was fetching coffee and keeping the crafts table stocked. They all seemed completely certain of a bright future in the business, and that this gig would get them there. I had a feeling the source of that confidence had just joined us.

She wore a goldenrod power suit that complimented her dark hair and brown skin perfectly. I'd never seen Sami dressed up. Not like this. Her hair was pulled back into a tight braid, which was a shame. I loved those dark, glossy curls. I wanted to gather them in my hands and tilt her face up to mine... *Knock it off, Colosi.*

"I better get over there," the kid said. He didn't wait for a response. I'd have to seek him out later and actually listen to whatever he'd been pitching. He deserved that much.

Sami sat with Kassi at her side. Desi was out of the country, according to one of the interns. Kassi and I got along. We'd worked well together and had each ended up with an armload of awards as a result. But Desi and I were pals. We'd hit it off almost immediately. I'd hoped she would help as I navigated the *Death Sucks* set, but she wasn't here. I hadn't pressed for details. Rumors spread like wildfire in this town.

"Ready to go?" Sami asked the room.

"Ready to go!" they answered with enthusiasm. Excitement all but crackled in the air, perhaps because this script was for the season finale. Television filming schedules could be grueling. This meant there was light at the end of the tunnel.

"I'm Samantha Augustine, show runner for *Death Sucks*."

The room burst into cheers and applause.

Sami fought a smile and lost. Her face shined. She loved these people. "I keep telling you, flattery will not get you a later call time."

I joined in the laughter, more out of surprise than anything else. I'd said something similar at my last table read. Kassi remembered. She glanced over and gave me a small smile.

"To my left we have the brilliant, and might I add, Oscar winning screenwriter, Kassandre Mevin."

More cheers, followed by chants of, "Kas-si! Kas-si!"

Kassi hid behind her script until they stopped. She wore her hair down, the better to shield her face. The attention of the room passed before she set the papers down. Sami leaned over and said something. Kassi nodded and scribbled a note on the first page of her script. The introductions went around the room. Everyone gave their name from department heads to interns. I did this on my sets because the table read was often where everyone met for the first time. This had a different effect. It gave everyone a voice. Sami did this to acknowledge every single person on her set. They knew it, and they loved her for it. Even an outsider like me could see that.

And then it was my turn. "Jarrod Colosi, guest director," I said.

"Oscar winning guest director," someone amended, and the applause grew. I waved it away. Something in Sami's expression told me she wanted to roll her eyes, but her face stayed under tight control, just like her hair.

A few more names and we were ready to begin. "*Death Sucks*, season six, episode twelve, 'Give Me Novacaine', written by Samantha Augustine." More cheers.

"Goodness, everyone is rowdy today," Sami said, but there was no heat to her words.

The name of the episode gave me hope. Music was my first love. Unfortunately, I could act better than I could sing, and my parents had paid for drama coaches, not vocal lessons. Sami was a music fan. It might not be part of her soul like it was with Desi, but a Green Day song for an episode title made me smile. We had common ground. If only she was willing to see it.

I made my notes on the script and waited for the room to empty out before approaching. It seemed that everyone was welcome to make suggestions. Sami listened to each and took notes. Kass hadn't budged from her seat, though I'd seen her glance at the door several times. She seemed determined to stay by Sami's side. If Desi were here, would she and Kassi form a wall to keep me away from Sami? I knew better than to try to split up the *tres amigas*. Sami glanced at her watch. Why did that motion seem contrived? "I have a call in three minutes."

"Don't you want my input on the script?" I asked.

Sami's eyebrows rose. "Put it in an email," she said. "We'll see you next week. Kass, I need you." Sami brushed past me. Kassi's wide eyes darted from me to Sami and back again, looking slightly apologetic as she hurried after her friend.

Show runners were always busy. I knew that, but over the years, Sami had turned avoiding me into a full on Olympic sport. She might have a call scheduled, or that might be an excuse. I was good at reading people, but I never could tell with her.

I hung around the set to get a look at the operation. Sets belonged to the crew. Even on my films, I had no illusions about that. I might bark orders, but I was just a traveler going through that space. It might feel like my domain, but it wasn't my home. The main rule was *stay out of the way*, so that was what I did. Once the equipment was set up, most people were more than happy to talk to me. I wanted everything to go smoothly for my episode of *Death Sucks,* and that meant knowing how things worked. When I'd signed on, I hadn't asked for the season finale. Any episode would have been fine. I would have waited until the next season, but I liked this timing better. By the time we'd wrapped on Desi's film, *Under the Water*, I'd already been planning to adapt Kassi's epic novel *Error of the Moon*. The schedule had been a nightmare, but we got it in under the wire for the awards season. The nominations rolled in. Sami had conveniently been on the east coast during the Oscars, and it bothered me more than I cared to admit that she hadn't been there to celebrate with us.

No one had ever affected me the way Sami did. I was the love 'em and leave 'em type. Women chased me. They found excuses to work near me and did their best to get my attention. Now I was the one following someone around like a lost puppy. It was ridiculous. The more Sami ignored me, the more I craved her attention. One more time, that's what I told myself. If I could be with her one more time, I'd get her out of my system and life would get back to normal. Work on my next project was eight weeks away. I would start early with the prep work, though I'd read the script, and it wasn't anything great. There would be a lot of green screens and CGI. Post production would take longer than the actual filming, but once it was done, we'd all make a ton of money. It would be a summer blockbuster. So why was I dreading the thought of it all?

The answer to that question strode toward me wearing a fake smile that did nothing to diffuse the flash of her eyes. Her heels clicked on the concrete in an irritated staccato. I might have masochistic tendencies, but, damn, that woman was glorious when she was angry. I didn't bother to fight my smile. Her eyebrows drew down, making her smile turn maniacal. It was a good look... if she wanted to play Chuckles the Clown's sidekick.

"Why, Mr. Colosi, you're still here," Sami said, her voice cheerful as her golden brown eyes shot daggers. "How fortuitous."

Maybe Sami thought this friendly routine was convincing, but one glance around told me that no one was fooled. The area cleared out faster than a beach during a thunderstorm.

"Indeed it is," I agreed. "Do you have a moment to go over the script? I just have a few notes."

"Certainly," she said, not missing a beat. She gripped her pen so tight, her knuckles had turned white. "Let's pop in here for a moment."

"Sir, there's no popping. Stay in the car," I said. It wasn't an exact quote, but I knew she'd get it.

Sami stared at me like I'd grown a second head.

"You're supposed to ask if I think there's a florist planning an assassination," I said.

She understood the reference. I was certain of it and equally certain that she would never give me the satisfaction of admitting it. "Would you like some water?" she asked, as if she thought I might need it.

"I'm good," I said. Sami didn't appreciate my humor. I followed her into a small office and considered my next move.

Sami shut the door. "Why are you here?"

"I-I'm directing an episode."

She drew in air through her nose. "I understand that, but why? Why the sudden urge to direct television? Don't you have another film scheduled?"

"I had some downtime. Lewis and I were golfing one day, and I mentioned how much I like the show."

Her eyes bored into me. "And who suggested directing an episode? Mr. Davies or you?"

I thought about it. "I don't know. Lewis said one of the producers was leaving to work on her own project. I volunteered to help out for a week or two." How had that turned into directing an episode? I wasn't sure. We'd started drinking on the second hole and I'd ridden home in the back of a town car, pleased with the idea of bringing part of Sami's fictional world to life. It didn't seem like such a great plan now.

"And did *Lewis* mention that I promote from within and already had someone ready to step in when Chanthou left?"

"He might have," I admitted. "I'm a little fuzzy on the details."

"Because you were drinking, perhaps?"

"Of course," I said. "Have you ever been on the links with Lewis? The man throws them back like..."

She lowered her chin and glared at me.

I realized my mouth was open and closed it. "I'll back out if you want me to."

"Perfect! And how do you think ol' *Lewis* would take that? The promotion department is already hyping the finale and our Oscar winning director." She managed to make my golden statue sound like something obscene.

"I don't understand. Isn't that good?" I said. "If people watch this finale, they'll probably go back and watch the rest."

"No, you don't understand," she said through tight lips. "Because all you have to do is call your pal who happens to be president of the network and go play a round of golf, and you just stumble into directing the biggest finale we've had yet."

"It'll be great, Sam, the script is excellent."

"I know it's excellent, Jarrod. I wrote it. I've been planning every detail leading to this episode for six seasons. And then you just waltz in here like a great white knight when you don't have a clue what it has taken to get to this point."

"I understand planning for a big finish," I said.

"Oh, really?" She snatched the script out of my hand. I'd rolled it like a newspaper. It was a bad habit, one I'd tried to break.

Sami scowled at the pages and tried to get them straight. "Here. I saw you make this note."

And here I thought she'd been ignoring me during the table read.

"This line that you want to cut? It's a reference back to the third episode of season five. It's important to tie up a plot line that we purposely left dangling. You understand nothing."

"Jon Snow," I finished for her. She didn't even crack a smile. "I'll catch up," I assured her. "If you'll let me watch what you've done so far..."

Her expression said that was not going to happen.

"Or send me the scripts? I can ask Mickey or her..."

"Their."

"Their assistant." I'd guessed at Mickey's pronouns and had gotten them wrong. Could it be any more obvious how out of place I was here? "To send me the scripts. I'll binge the past seasons and read everything from this one. I won't mess up your show, I promise." I gave her wide, earnest eyes.

She softened just a tiny bit. "You think you can just do some homework and be all bright eyed and ready to take on everything a week later? Is that how things work in your world?"

"Ah, but I'm in your world now," I said, leaning in just a little. "If I do all my homework, will you let me stay a while?"

"I hate you," she said. There was no venom in the phrase. It was almost a sigh.

I didn't fight my grin. "No, you don't."

She rolled those beautiful golden eyes, spun on her heel, opened the door and strode away. Since there was no one around to see, I let myself watch the way that pencil skirt hugged her pert ass. I'd hate to see her walk away if the view was anything less than spectacular.

Chapter Four

SAMI

*T*hat man. That damn, insufferable man and the effect he had on my body.

"You know, sometimes, I want to slap that cocky smile right off your face."

The smile had widened instead of diminishing. "Go ahead. I dare you."

I'd closed the distance between us, my hand raised and ready to strike. Jarrod had caught my wrist and kissed me instead. Damn him.

It had happened the night of Desi's birthday, the wrap party for her film *Under the Water* at Jarrod's house. One of our favorite bands, Psychodelia, had played, courtesy of Jaime Ruster, an old friend of Desi's and Jarrod's. I'd enjoyed myself thoroughly, drinking a little and dancing a lot. And there had been Jarrod, his dark eyes trained on me the whole time. It had been the perfect evening, and I had run out of excuses.

"Stick around, and I'll give you the nickel tour," he said. Maybe other women could hold their resolve when faced with that wicked smile, but I couldn't.

"What's the price if we skip the car collection, two cents?" I quipped.

"So you don't want to see the back seat of my '63 Lincoln?" He was entirely too sure of himself.

That's when I'd threatened to slap him and my hands ended up in his hair while he kissed me instead. I knew there was heat between us, but didn't expect the fire that scorched my veins when our lips met. He was polite, not demanding, until I opened to him. Then he seemed intent on completely possessing my mouth. We were both breathing hard when he broke away and trailed kisses over my cheek, down to my neck.

"How about my bedroom?" he murmured into that space behind my earlobe, turning my skin to gooseflesh.

"Yes."

Jarrod drew back, surprised. "Yes?" Maybe he wasn't so confident after all.

"Yes," I answered simply. I'd had a few drinks, but I wasn't drunk. I knew what I was doing. One night, a bit of fun, and I could stop thinking about Jarrod Colosi once and for all. I'd imagined this since I was a teenager, and he was a television heartthrob. What was the point of working in Hollywood if I couldn't cross a few celebrity crushes off my list? Desi had gotten Patrick Flannigan, and if the way he looked at her was any indication, he'd be around for a while. What was the harm in me spending one night with Jarrod Colosi?

His bedroom was what I expected, modern, sparsely furnished and decorated in dark greys with floor to ceiling windows overlooking the valley. The huge television was disguised as a framed painting on the wall. It provided the only pop of color in the room.

"If you're going to do that, you should pick someone other than Jackson Pollock," I said, nodding to the screen.

"You need to see the texture of his work. Two dimensions can't do it justice."

"I'll choose something more suitable for next time," Jarrod said. His eyes were so dark, I could barely tell see where his pupils ended and irises began. "Did you come here to critique my interior decorating?"

I arched an eyebrow at him, accepting the challenge. "No, that's not why."

"Sami," he sort of growled my name, and damn if that didn't send heat shooting straight through me. We fell together in a tangle of tongues and limbs. Our clothes disappeared, not by spontaneous combustion as they should have, but through a series of awkward tugs and lots of repositioning. He guided my hand between my legs before looping his fingers under the elastic of my lace panties and pulling them down over my hips. "Touch yourself," Jarrod said. "Show me what you do late at night when you're thinking about me."

"Who says I ever think about you?" I asked, but my fingers were already moving, delving into my pussy, finding that magic spot that could make everything else go away. "Voyeur," I accused.

"Yup," Jarrod agreed, his dark gaze locked on my fingers. I spread my legs a little to give him a better view.

"What if I can't come with you watching?" I asked, my voice breathy. That delicious tension coiled inside me.

Jarrod chuckled. "Hate to break it to you, beautiful, but you're going to come lots of times with me watching."

I bit my lip.

"But, if you can't do it, I suppose I'll give you a kiss and tuck you in for the night."

"I thought we were going to fuck!" The fire coursing through my veins made that come out more indignant than I'd planned.

Jarrod laughed again. "Mmm, there you are. See, naughty

girls know how to get themselves off, and only naughty girls get to fuck. Good girls, the prim and proper ones, get tucked in and left alone to sleep it off until they come back to their senses."

That was a dig, the "prim and proper" bit. I wasn't about to let him get away with it. Jarrod had a reputation, not just as a Hollywood bad boy. "Where I come from, naughty girls get spanked," I said.

His face brightened with interest. "Are you into that?"

"Maybe."

"Ms. Augustine, are you saying that you want me to put you across my lap and spank you like the bad girl you are?"

"Silly boy," I said. "Haven't you realized by now that bad girls *like* to be spanked?"

I would have laughed at his dumbfounded expression had that tension inside me not been coiled so damn tight.

"I won't stop with your luscious ass," he threatened. "I'll paddle that naughty pussy too."

I lost my rhythm. My fingers skittered to a halt, and I stared at him.

"Ever try that?"

I shook my head.

"D'you want to?"

I nodded breathlessly.

"Say it. Tell me what you want me to do, and I swear, I'll follow your every command."

My hand moved again of its own accord, harder, faster than before. "I want you to put me over your lap and spank me." I panted the words.

"Tell me where."

God, I could probably get off just listening to that low, dangerous voice. "My ass and my p-pussy." The tension broke like a dark cloud finally releasing rain. Jarrod was next to me in an instant, his fingers thrust inside me, prolonging my orgasm. I rode his hand. There was no holding back. Not this time. Heat burst through me again. This time, he swallowed my cries with his mouth over mine.

"I knew you'd be wild." I could hear his grin in his voice. "We're going to have so much fun."

I could barely focus enough to realize what was happening, and then suddenly, he sat on the edge of the bed with me lying across his lap. I should have felt vulnerable, naked as I was, but he was naked, too. I could feel his erection. He was enjoying this. I rubbed against him.

Jarrod smoothed his hand over the curve of my backside. "Tell me to stop, and I will."

"You haven't started yet," I pointed out.

"I'm serious, Sam."

I looked over my shoulder. "If at any point I don't like what you're doing, I will let you know." There had to be trust on both sides of this equation. We both understood that.

Whatever Jarrod saw on my face must have satisfied him. He shifted so his knee parted my legs. I arched into his hand. He brought it down in a way that was more sound than substance, first on one cheek, then the other, then lower, between my legs. *Oh, hello.* It wasn't much, but that light contact on my pussy shot through me like lightning. That thunderstorm was building again. I could feel him watching me, judging my reactions. I tried to encourage him with every fiber of my being. *More. Harder.* I liked some pain mixed in, but this wasn't pain. It was pure pleasure, and I ached for more. My bottom heated, but it was nothing compared to the rest of me. My core ached and throbbed. I was soaked and so damn close. Jarrod seemed to sense that. He flipped me onto the bed and crouched between my legs. The flat of his hand made contact with my mons once, twice. The third time, I flew apart, and he dove in. His tongue soothed away any sting and delved through my swollen folds. My hands both found their way to his dark hair. I spread my legs wider and rode his face shamelessly, pulling him tighter, demanding more attention until I felt certain I would die from pleasure. I cried out more than once. I might have even screamed his name, though I'd never admit that.

I fell back, and he raised his head. His hair looked sexy, all mussed like that. His face was flushed and glistening, his lips dark red and swollen. I wanted to kiss him. As if reading my mind, he crawled next to me and covered my mouth with his. I tasted myself on him, and that just made everything hotter.

"You're a goddess," he said. His eyes burned into mine.

I searched for a snappy comeback and came up empty. He leaned over me and fumbled in the nightstand drawer for a condom. I liked that he checked with me, holding it up and arching an eyebrow instead of just assuming. Nevertheless, I gave him a "duh" look and opened the foil packet.

"Lie back," I said.

He did, and I took a moment to admire his taught body. I'd never been into body builders. Jarrod's body was cut, but not bulky. He didn't have a large frame, and was lean like me. I ran my fingers through the smattering of dark hair on his pecs and felt him tremble. It wasn't easy for him to lie still and let me take over. I recognized that and exploited it. I traced his abs, not super clearly defined, but they were definitely present, circled his navel and followed that path of dark hair leading lower. He groaned. I gave him a teasing smile and gripped his cock in my fist. He jerked and probably would have flown off the bed if I hadn't pinned him in place with my frown. Two could play at this game.

"Sami," he whispered through gritted teeth.

"Tell me what you want, naughty boy," I purred. I jerked him up and down twice in quick succession before resuming my slow caress.

He whimpered. Oh, this was fun. "Please."

Jarrod Colosi could beg. Who knew? "Please what?" I assumed my best innocent expression; all the while sliding my hand up, twirling over his sensitive cock head and sliding it back down again.

"You're killing me."

"You want me to stop?" I didn't release him completely, but the feather light touch couldn't have helped.

"No, Sam! Don't stop!"

"But you don't seem to be enjoying yourself." I pouted and batted my eyelashes at him.

"I want to be inside you. Please, Sami, I want you to fuck me."

I smiled. "Now was that so hard?" I gave him one last squeeze and rolled the condom in place. The wrapper landed on the hardwood floor with our discarded clothes. There would be time for tidiness later. I straddled him and rubbed myself over the length of him. He started to reach for me and seemed to think better of it, reaching for the top of the mattress and casting his eyes skyward instead.

"Jarrod," I murmured his name. "Don't you want to watch?" I teased the corner of my mouth with one finger.

His forehead crinkled in consternation, but his eyes locked on my hand. I trailed it down, over my chin, between my breasts, over my stomach and lower, to where I had him positioned right where I wanted him to be. He groaned again as I slid slowly onto him. His muscles twitched like he wanted to move, but he let me maintain control. I rather liked him for that. Once he was fully seated inside me, his patience ran out. He rose up and wrapped himself around me. His hips flexed, and I felt him move deep inside me. That was okay. I was done playing. I plunged my fingers into his hair and pulled him to me. His arms wrapped up over my back and gripped my shoulders so he could drive deeper. I wouldn't last long in this position. He probably wouldn't either. I leaned back so he was more likely to hit that perfect spot inside me. He took the opportunity to catch my nipple between his teeth. The sharp contact ricocheted through me. I gripped him tighter. He gave my other breast the same treatment. I exploded again.

Jarrod leaned over me, brushing my hair off my forehead. We were still joined in the most intimate way. He waited for me to focus before his hips moved again. He hadn't been kidding about watching me come. He did that a few more times, watching me fly apart and come floating back to earth, checking in before continuing. I'd heard that he was kinky, but there had been nothing about studying Tantra in the rumors. Had I really thought that he wouldn't be able to last long? He kept pushing me, and I couldn't bring myself to complain until finally, covered in sweat and nearing exhaustion, I used his hair like a handle to get those dark eyes to meet mine.

"Jarrod," I said. "It's okay to let go." I didn't really give him a choice. I'd been doing Kegel exercises for years. I used those muscles to grip him tight. I was a little sore, but it was a good kind of ache, like pushing to the end of a great work out.

Jarrod's eyes widened. "Wha-?"

I controlled the rhythm now. His thrusts grew erratic as my hips rose to meet his. I gripped his ass and guided him how I wanted, faster, harder. His whole body tensed and he shouted, sounding surprised. He collapsed onto me, and I held him, petting his hair and rubbing soothing circles into his back.

"Holy shit." He rolled off me and lay on his back, staring at the ceiling.

"That's one way or putting it," I agreed.

He turned to look at me. His hand cupped the side of my face, and he smiled. "You're a goddess."

"So you said."

"Stay the night?"

"No." I said it gently, but that didn't seem to lessen his disappointment. I got dressed. He watched me the whole time. "I had a good time," I said and leaned across the bed to brush my lips over his.

He looked so cute sitting there, all rumpled and confused. I was tempted to snap a picture.

"I did too," he finally said.

I found my shoes, a pair of spiky heels that Desi called "fuck me shoes" and held them rather than tottering around trying to put them on.

"Are you okay to drive? I think the town cars have all gone."

"I only had two drinks, and that was..." I looked at my watch. "Seven hours ago. Wow. Time flies, right?"

"Yeah."

"I'll see you around." And I would see him. That might be a problem, or it might not. I wasn't sure which.

"Sami," he called when I had nearly reached the door.

I turned back. "Yes?"

He seemed at a loss as to what to say. "I'll see you around," he finally repeated my words.

I nodded and walked out the door.

Chapter Five

JARROD

I hadn't been kidding about the homework. I knew about *Death Sucks*. No convention was complete without at least one panel for the show. I'd seen an episode here and there, but I'd never sat down and really watched it. It wasn't completely necessary to do so now. The consistency came from having the same three writers on every episode. But I'd worked in television. A director could change a lot even without rewriting the script. I didn't want to screw this up.

I started watching with that thought in mind. My ego didn't want anyone, especially Sami, to say I couldn't do a good job directing a television show. My view changed quickly as the genius of the show became clear. It stopped being about me as my focus shifted to the show and the hope that I was a worthy captain, no matter how temporary, to steer that ship.

I binged the first five seasons over the course of three days and quickly understood the fan following. The show was clever and fun. More than that, the philosophies of the writers shined through like beacons. Having worked on scripts by all three women, I could tell who had penned the episode without checking the credits. There was a period during season two where Sami must have been busy with production, because her name only appeared in the byline twice. Kassi was the Alexander Hamilton of the group, writing an average of thirteen episodes each season. I read the scripts from the current season, but I needed an inside source to let me know how to navigate set life. I called Desi.

The phone rang several times before she answered.

"Hey, Jarrod." It sounded more like a sigh.

There was a lot of noise in the background. "Where are you?" I asked.

"Iceland."

"Ugh. Why?"

"What do you mean, 'ugh'? It's beautiful here, if a bit frigid. Jarrod, what the hell are you doing?"

"What do you mean?"

"Why are you on our set? Are you crazy?"

"I'm directing an episode. You've had guest directors before." I'd recognized several names in the credits.

She sighed again. The background noise diminished. She must have been walking away. "Did you bother to check who was lined up to direct that episode before you signed on?"

"What? No. Why would I do that? It was available." But she was right. It would only be available if the scheduled director got bumped. And this wasn't just any episode. It was a finale. "Who was it?" I asked.

"Sami."

"Fuck me," I said.

"Yeah, I wouldn't count on that happening any time soon," Desi said. "She's raging."

That last word had an Irish lilt to it. "You've been around Patrick," I teased, trying to lighten the mood.

It didn't work. "I'll be back on set Monday, but let's get one thing straight. Sami outranks you."

"I know," I said. Desi, Kass and Sami had been friends since college. I could be friendly with all of them, but my chances of getting anyone in that squad to take my side were precisely zero. "I can't back out, or the network will be pissed." Sami had made that much clear, and she was right. The blowback would land right on her. "I just don't want to screw it up. You can help me do that, surely. I mean, it's for the good of the show, right?"

Desi seemed to consider this. "What precisely are you asking for?"

"Tell me about set life."

Chapter Six

SAMI

There were usually a half dozen projects on my "to do" list, but I had wrapped up a lot of loose ends in preparation for directing the season finale. My other two shows had already wrapped. I still produced both of them, but *Death Sucks* had been my pet project for a while now. Mickey handled most of the day-to-day stuff on other series, leaving me to worry about the scripts and story continuity. I was copied on most decisions and had final veto power, but had never needed to exercise it. With all that, I found myself in the uncomfortable position of having little to do. I could have gone next door to my cousin's house and collected my daughter early. I told myself that would only disrupt her routine. Besides, I wasn't in a suitable mood to be around adults, let alone a three-year-old.

I opened my tablet and scrolled through emails. What I found there brightened my mood dramatically. *Green light for* Nevermind. *Let's meet to discuss particulars.* I stared at the screen. I'd felt this before, excitement and trepidation in equal measures coursing through my veins, making my thoughts freeze until everything blurred but the words on the screen . *Green light for* Nevermind. We'd been in negotiations for well over a year. I'd worried that Kassi's film, *Error of the Moon*, would conflict with the scheduling and we'd both be off set at the same time. Jarrod had stunned everyone, including most Hollywood insiders, by taking advantage of long summer days and pushing the schedule to the limits. Why was I thinking about Jarrod? I focused on the screen instead. If we could start pre-production soon, we could be on location by September. The proposal, which Mickey and I had laid out in great detail, included shooting in Berlin through the fall and winter. That would mean living in Germany for almost six months. Carmen was supposed to start preschool in the fall. International travel could only help her education. There had to be English speaking preschools in Germany.

The front door opened. Lucia entered with Carmen and Maia in tow. "So you are here. Carmen said you were home, but I thought you'd come over to see us if you were."

"Mommy!" Carmen ran to me before I could respond to Lucia's thinly veiled complaint.

"Hi, baby," I said, lifting her onto my lap. She chattered about her day and games she and Maia had played.

"Well?" Lucia said.

"I didn't want to interrupt dinner," I said.

"Because of course, you couldn't eat with us."

"I didn't want to be a bother." Lucia's face told me what she thought of that. "Besides, I wasn't hungry, and I had some work to finish."

"You always have work," Carmen said, reminding me that there were little ears listening to every word we said.

"That's true, but now it's time to turn everything off and spend time with you," I said.

My devices would be back on as soon as I tucked Carmen into bed, but she didn't need to know that. Lucia sat down across from me. She wasn't finished yet.

"Carmen, why don't you and Maia go into the den and play a game? I'll be there in a little bit." They would be engrossed in Mario Kart within minutes. I waited until I heard the music from the other room before turning back to face Lucia.

"What's this?" she demanded, holding up my tablet. "Berlin? As in Germany? Are you going to Germany now? When were you going to tell me?"

"We just got the funding. Nothing is set yet. You know how these things work. There's a whole lot of nothing and then things finally start moving." Even then, projects fell through as often as they went forward. I didn't want to jinx myself.

"And when it does start moving, you just expect me to move to Berlin too?"

"I was going to ask," I said.

"Sure you were." She harrumphed. "I can't just move to Germany, Sami. I have a life, you know. Maia has school. She has friends."

"I know. I would arrange everything."

"You'd have your assistant arrange everything." Lucia scoffed.

"Of course. You want it done right, don't you?" Evan organized a good portion of my life. He'd been my assistant since before I created *Death Sucks*. I didn't plan much of anything without his help.

"I won't do it," she said.

"Okay," I said. Lucia often said she wouldn't do something, then changed her mind later.

"Okay," she imitated me. "Like it doesn't matter one way or the other. You don't appreciate me at all."

"That's not true, and you know it."

"It is. I raise your child for you. I keep her all day and

overnight and for days at a time while you travel. I'm with her more than you are."

"And you're pretty well paid for it too," I said.

"That's always your answer, isn't it? Throw money at a problem." She flicked her wrists, flinging the imaginary money in the air. "Well, that won't work this time. Money and material things won't mean as much to Carmen as time spent with her mother."

As if I didn't know that. As if I didn't feel guilty about leaving her all the time. I felt equally guilty leaving the studio, though. I wasn't one of those people who could sing silly songs and play with toys to amuse a child all day and still be sane at the end of it all.

"You heard her. She knows you care more about your job than your own daughter."

Fury rose in me. I had created a television empire, and Lucia had the audacity to call it a *job*? It was the last bit that cut deep, though. As if anything could possibly be more important than Carmen. I wanted to shout, but the girls were in the next room. Instead, I kept my voice low and spoke through my gritted teeth. "And where would she get that idea from, Luce? Her other friends have parents who work. Does she think those parents don't care about their children, or is that something you only say about me?"

"You have no idea what it is to care for a child." Lucia's argument pivoted rather than admit I'd scored a point. "All your life, if you didn't want to do something, you could always manipulate someone else into doing it for you. It's my fault. I was your puppet for a long time, but I'm not anymore. I have plans too, you know."

"For heaven's sake, you go through this routine every few months. Just tell me what you want. You need more free time? Want me to take both the girls for a weekend so you can have some alone time? A day at the spa? What?"

"Screw you, Sami. Don't patronize me."

I sighed. "I've heard that before too."

"I'm leaving."

"Fine. We'll talk about this later."

"No, I'm leaving. I'm taking Maia, and we're going to visit Mama for a while."

"You just visited her over the holidays."

"That was for the holiday break. This is because I need a break from *you*. Watch your own kid for a while and maybe you'll realize all that I do for you."

"I do realize everything you do for me," I said.

"No, you don't." She shook her head emphatically. The gesture reminded me of Carmen in the middle of a temper tantrum. "But you will. Though I suppose you'll just find someone else to take care of her. You have plenty of money for that."

"Luce, come on."

"I'm serious," she said. "You need a reality check. I'll be back when I feel like coming back."

"I suppose you want me to pay for your flight too."

Her eyes narrowed. "I have my own money, Sami. I'm not completely dependent on you. You don't own me. Maia and I will go on a road trip."

"In the car I pay for."

"Which you never let me forget," Lucia said. "This has been a long time coming. Enjoy your time with your daughter." She raised her voice in order to be heard over the game. "Maia, come on! We're leaving."

"Just a minute," Maia called.

"Now!"

"Mom, we're in the middle of a race!"

"Right this minute! Don't make me come in there."

Maia emerged, her face mutinous, but she kept her mouth closed. Smart girl.

Lucia grabbed her daughter's hand, stalked out of the house, and slammed the door behind her.

Carmen climbed onto my lap. "Was Auntie Lucy mad?"

"Probably," I said.

"Did I do something bad?"

I looked down into her face. Her eyes were especially similar to mine, almost identical. "No, baby. She's upset with me."

"Did you do something bad?"

"No, not bad, just... It's complicated. You didn't get to finish playing Mario Kart. Do you want me to play with you?"

"Can you stay on the road this time?"

"Oh, trash talking daughter!" I said, tickling her. Carmen giggled. I picked her up and threw her over my shoulder. She kicked her feet and squealed. She was right though, I couldn't stay on the damn course. The turtle shells and bananas were only partly to blame.

Chapter Seven

SAMI

Maybe I did take Lucia for granted. I certainly didn't expect her car to be gone the next day. She must have left at the crack of dawn. I wondered how she could have arranged it all so quickly. Maybe I wasn't the only one who had been up late last night.

"Where's Auntie Lucy?" Carmen asked as we stood on the porch and I stared stupidly at the locked door. I had a key, of course, but it was home on the hook in the kitchen. I never needed it in the morning. Lucia was always home, always ready to take my daughter and keep watch over her for the day.

"That's right, she and Maia were going on a trip. I forgot. Silly mommy."

Carmen looked up at me with wide eyes. "They went without me?"

I knew that look. She was mere moments from bursting into tears. "That's okay," I said brightly. "I'll stay home from work. We can spend the whole day together."

"But Maia went too. Who's going to play with me?"

"I will."

"No!" she said, tears filling her eyes and rolling down her cheeks. "I want Maia. I want Auntie Lucy!"

Before I could say anything more, she sat down on the porch and sobbed like her heart was broken. I scooped her up to carry her back to our house, but she was having none of it. A full on tantrum ensued. I carried her under my arm like a sack of potatoes, careful to avoid flailing fists and feet. Three was a wonderful age. Would four be any better? I set Carmen on her bed. "When you're ready, I'll be in the kitchen. I have to make some calls, but then I'll be ready to play with you."

She hid her face under her pillow and pounded her feet angrily on the mattress. I should have taken her shoes off. Now the sheets would need to be changed.

I refused to give Lucia the satisfaction of hearing from me. She had probably just gone out for breakfast and then went shopping. Whatever it took to put the fear of god into me. Well, I could take a Friday off. I'd end up working remotely, but I'd done that before. Everything would be fine.

By eleven o'clock, I was at my wit's end. I turned on one of the Shrek movies. It didn't matter which, and left Carmen staring at the screen. I never did that. Television time was as regulated as video games. But who was I kidding? I rarely spent all day trying to entertain Carmen. Who knew she was so demanding? *Just like you.* I could hear my mother say. I called my mother.

"So, I hear you are taking care of your daughter for a change." So much for niceties.

"I always take care of my daughter," I said, bristling. "Did Lucia arrive yet?"

"You don't, and you never have. It's time you take responsibility."

I pinched the bridge of my nose. Responsibility? Was my mother really talking to me about responsibility? I'd paid my own way through college and supported myself ever since. I ran three different television shows, for heavens' sake, but I didn't take responsibility?

"You work all the time. It's a wonder Carmen even knows who you are. What are you working for? That fancy house? That nice car?"

"I suppose your fancy house and nice car were supplied by the sugar plum fairy," I said before I could stop myself. My mother and Auntie Tianna each occupied one side of a sweet duplex in Oregon. The neighborhood where Lucia and I grew up had gone downhill, and it hadn't been that nice to begin with. This was better, safer, and they were close enough to keep an eye on each other while still having their own space.

"That's quite enough of that. Lucy has dreams too. She needs her own life beyond taking care of your child."

"Not just my child," I said.

"At least Maia has a father," my mother said.

"Here we go," I groaned. Lucia was a single mother too, but she'd been married when she had Maia. Her husband had been useless on just about every front. She'd divorced him when she grew tired of caring for an overgrown child in addition to a toddler. She'd also called me after a few months of living with Auntie Tia and asked if there was any job I could give her to get her out of her mother's house. I'd been pregnant with Carmen and already terrified of what came next. To my mother's thinking, at least there was a name on Maia's birth certificate above the word "father." Carmen's said "unknown."

"You don't even get child support," my mother was saying.

"I don't need it, either," I said. I knew how to handle money. I'd learned that as soon as I started earning it. I learned how to invest and make it grow. Kassi, Desi, and I had all been in the work-study program at college. We'd watched our grades carefully to keep our scholarships, and watched our bank accounts just as carefully. That bonded us together in those early days as much as anything else.

"What are you going to tell Carmen when she asks about her father? Are you going to make up a story like you do every week for the TV?"

"I've got to go now, mom."

"You should call Lucy and apologize."

"For what, exactly?"

"For taking her for granted. For treating her like she's disposable, the way you treat everyone. You exhaust people, Samantha. You wear them out. Everything has to be about you. It's too much. *You're* too much sometimes."

I looked at the ceiling. No help there. "I think Carmen is calling me. Bye, Mom. Love you." I ended the call without waiting for her response. My mother always knew exactly which buttons to push. It must have been a family trait, because Auntie Tia drove Lucia crazy, too. As kids, we'd always wanted to swap parents.

I did my best over the weekend. I really did. For two days straight, I played Candy Land, Chutes and Ladders, several versions of Mario, put together puzzles, made up quests for Carmen, and described dragons for her to slay. When she decided that she would rather keep the dragons as pets and overthrow the rulers who sent her on the quest, I approved heartily. There were bright moments like that, and then there were the meltdowns that made me question if I was cut out for parenting at all.

Tears streamed down Carmen's face. She had worked herself into a full blown tantrum when I said that no, we could not go to the playground. Never mind that it was dark outside, and we were both exhausted. This, in addition to the battle over dinner, was apparently the final straw. "I hate you!" she shouted.

Ouch. All jokes about "threenagers" aside, that cut right

through me. I knew I couldn't be a mother without hearing that at least a few times. I just didn't expect it so soon. None of the responses I'd prepared, *Well, that's your prerogative*, or *Then I must be doing something right*, were appropriate to say to a child who had not yet turned four. Carmen breathed heavily as she waited for my response. Her tiny hands were balled into fists. Her whole body was rigid.

I took a deep breath and tried to mentally step back. "Okay, I understand you're angry with me. Can you tell me why?"

"You don't care about me!"

"Carmen, I love you more than anyone else in the whole world." I tried to pull her close, but she wouldn't let me. She was crying too hard. "Baby, come here," I said.

"No!" She crumpled into a ball.

I joined her on the floor. Finally, she let me hold her.

I waited until her sobs slowed to sniffles, rubbing her back and letting her tears soak the front of my shirt. She leaned against me, limp and defeated.

"Why do you think I don't care about you?" I finally asked.

"You don't want anyone to know about me. Everyone thinks Auntie Lucy is my mommy."

That didn't sound like something she'd come up with on her own, but I let it go. "Remember how we talked about reporters and how they want to know a lot about me because I work in TV?" I asked.

She nodded.

"Well, they get to see a lot of my life. They get to write about it in their articles and talk about what I do and where I go. But this part, the mommy part of my life, that's just for you. The reporters can't have that part of me because it's just yours. Understand? I'm your mommy and no one else's. I know I'm away a lot and you don't like that, and maybe you'd rather be with Auntie Lucy when you're angry with me. It's okay to feel that way. Maybe when you're mad at Auntie Lucy, you'd rather be with me?"

"I always want to be with you, but you're never here." Carmen sulked.

"You know I have a job, baby. That's how we get to live in this nice house with Auntie Lucy nearby. I work with Auntie Desi and Auntie Kass."

"Why can't you work here?" she asked. "Lonnie's mommy works at home. She wears a hat, and that means he can't make any noise because she's really busy."

I smiled a little. "I have a different kind of job than Lonnie's mommy. I have to be on set to tell everyone what to do next, or they will spend the whole day standing around and there would be no TV show."

"Do lots of people like your TV show?" she asked.

"They do. Remember the pictures I showed you from the convention with all the people who watch the show?"

She nodded. "Tell you what," I said. "You can come to the set with me tomorrow and see what I do all day.

"I can?"

I'd spent the weekend with one eye on Lucia's driveway, thinking that she'd be back before I returned to work on Monday. Surely, she and Auntie Tia would get on each other's nerves, and Lucia would come home. The truth was, I missed her. Most of my friends were childless workaholics. Lucia was the only person I could compare mom notes with. How did Lucia respond when Maia said, "I hate you"? Or was Lucia so perfect that Maia would never say such an awful thing? I looked out the window at Lucia's house. Not a single light cut through the darkness.

"You'll have to stay where I tell you," I said. "Otherwise, you could get hurt."

"I'll be good," Carmen said, all hurt feelings over the playground forgotten.

"Do you remember what the loud buzzer means?"

"We all have to be quiet, like mice," Carmen answered promptly. She had visited the set before, not for the whole day, but long enough to see what went happened there. It would be all right for a day, but not much longer. If Lucia didn't come back, I'd have to make other arrangements.

Chapter Eight

JARROD

Sami hadn't returned any of my messages over the weekend, but that was okay. She couldn't avoid me forever. Desi wouldn't talk to me about Sami, but she did give me plenty of information about everyone else. Not gossip. That wasn't her style, but I knew who followed which sports team and what fandom to reference to encourage smiles of recognition. It was little details like that which made Desi a pleasure to be around. She could talk to anyone because she listened to everyone. I did my best to emulate that.

I was discussing the parallel universes of *Star Trek Discovery* with a grip when he looked past me. "Uh-oh."

I glanced over my shoulder. There was Sami, flanked by Desi and Kassi. "What?"

"Their t-shirts are coordinated. That means they're a united front."

"I don't understand." Weren't they always united?

"I have to go do a thing." He hurried away.

I turned to face the trio. Sami's shirt featured a woman in a crown and an eyepatch. "Ovary up, bitches" was scrawled across the bottom. Desi's looked like a standard alumni shirt, but I had never heard of Brakebills University. Kassi's was souvenir style reading, "Someone went to Fillory, and all I got was this lousy t-shirt." I didn't see how they were coordinated. They didn't make any sense to me at all.

"Eyes up, if you please," Sami said wryly.

"Where is Brakebills University?" I asked.

"Upstate New York," Kassi deadpanned.

Sami smirked. Desi coughed into her hand, "Muggle."

Great. "Good morning to you too," I sighed. United front, indeed. "Would you like to go over my notes before we start blocking, just in case there's anything you don't like?"

We ended up in a small conference room. I tried to ignore the way they sat together on one side of the table, facing me. Sami's expression was tight and unreadable. Kassi kept her eyes on her script. Desi seemed more amused than anything else. I sighed and opened my script.

Lots of things, like which scenes were to be filmed on which day and in what order, had to be laid out ahead of time. I'd done that and gotten it to everyone at the end of the previous week. The crew needed time to plan, and it was only fair to let the talent know which lines to study. *Death Sucks* shot on a shorter schedule than most shows, five days of filming per episode instead of seven or eight. It meant longer days, but everyone got the weekends off. From what I had gathered, every person on set appreciated that schedule. In order to shoot so quickly, they had to be a word perfect set. The final version of the script came out on Friday and there were no last minute changes. I relied heavily on adlibs on my film sets, but I was willing to play by their rules. It was my interpretation of the script that I wanted the writers to approve. I had a reputation for finishing ahead of schedule, and because of one bit of information which Desi had let slip, I was determined to do that this week too. I had a plan for everyone's last day on set had already enlisted some co-conspirators to help with it.

Sami set the tone for this set, but right along with her was the first person on the call sheet. In this case, it was the lead actor, Linh Trach. She had just won a Golden Globe for her work on the series. It didn't take watching the first five seasons for me to see why. I knew casting directors who would bend over backwards to accommodate Linh's television schedule if it meant getting her in a film. Would Sami forgive me if I helped with that? Probably not.

The morning went well. I fell into the rhythm of blocking a scene, rehearsing it, resetting everything and shooting it. The actors were all brilliant, getting most scenes in two or three takes. We reshot from different angles and moved on. There were the occasional flubbed lines and giggle fits, but that was par for the course.

In between two scenes, the call rang out, "Dance break!" Desi had warned me about this particular routine. It was a good way to get everyone moving and shake off any cobwebs. I was thinking about enacting it on my own sets. Watching burly grips do the Safety Dance like a carefully coordinated flash mob made one hell of an impression.

Lunch time rolled around, and it was like waking out of a dream. I'd been too focused on the filming to look for Sami. An intern told me I could find her in the writers' room. A sign on the door made me hesitate with my hand raised to knock.

Writers at work! Do not disturb except in case of emergency. The following constitutes an emergency:

1. The building is on fire.

2. The zombie apocalypse has begun.

3. Alien spaceships have landed.

4. You come bearing gifts (and are not Greek).

5. You are delivering food or candy.

I had an intern getting me food from catering, so I didn't have to waste time in line. From what I understood, there was always a lot of candy in this particular room, and some of my ancestors did come from Greece, so I chose to ignore the sign. I'd been able to hear some chatter through the door, including what sounded like a child's voice. It all went silent when I knocked.

Desi answered the door, only opening it a little and blocking most of my view of the room. Food aromas wafted out. It smelled great. "Hey, Jarrod."

"Hey." I tried to peer past her. "Can I come in?"

"Sorry, but no one's allowed in here." She pointed to the sign.

"Seriously? I thought we were friends." That wasn't precisely fair, but neither was this girls' club game they kept playing.

Desi shrugged. "Chicks before dicks."

That made me laugh. "So that's how it is."

"That's how it is."

"We're still jamming later though, right?"

"Of course," Desi said, like that was a silly question to ask.

I spotted Kassi. "Kass? Help me out?"

Kassi shook her head. "Sisters before misters."

I heard a snorted laugh from within that had to be Sami. It was followed by a high giggle. "Who all is in there?"

"Gotta go. Later, Jarrod," Desi said, closing the door.

"If anyone needs me, I'll just be out here making your script come to life," I called through the door, even though I knew it wouldn't help. *Chicks before dicks.* I laughed again. We could play games. I liked games. I was good at them too.

Chapter Nine

SAMI

A set was no place for a child. I was the first to admit that under normal circumstances. These weren't normal circumstances, though. I kept waiting to hear from Lucia. She didn't call. I had to face reality. She would come back eventually, but even then, she might not want to take care of Carmen anymore. I had to make other arrangements. I looked at my daughter, sitting on Kassi's lap, listening to a story made up on the fly about photos they'd found on the internet. Carmen loved Lucia and Maia. It would hurt her to lose them. And if we moved to Germany for six months? Maybe I was selfish for even considering it.

As intended, Carmen fell asleep on Kassi's lap. We transferred her to a couch and dimmed the lights. I was accustomed to working with just my laptop screen for light. Desi and Kass had obligations elsewhere, and I had pages of emails to answer.

The novelty of the set had kept Carmen occupied during the morning. I'd brought toys and had videos to watch and an educational video game console. Our writers' room, mostly shut down and packed away by now, looked like a playroom with toys and snacks scattered on most of the surfaces and floor. We ate in the room all the time, but that wasn't the same. I'd have to get a gift for the cleaning crew, something better than the usual end of season swag basket. As the afternoon wore on, Carmen's patience grew thin. Kassi had to leave, and Desi was busy elsewhere. I did something I'd always tried not to do and took advantage of the interns who were all too eager to do anything I asked.

This is so unprofessional, I scolded myself as I hurried to the other side of the lot to resolve yet another emergency. I returned to find my latest intern victim leaning against the wall outside the room, typing furiously on her phone.

"Why are you out here?" I asked.

"She wanted 'alone time.' I don't think she likes me."

"She's three." I worked hard to keep from snapping the words. "She doesn't get to be in a room unsupervised."

"Don't worry. It's only been a few minutes."

I opened the door. The room was empty.

Chapter Ten

JARROD

There was some time between scenes while the crew set up and the talent visited wardrobe and makeup. I had the choice between sticking around to be hit up for advice by a few more aspiring directors and escaping for twenty minutes to check my messages. I chose the latter and headed to my temporary office to dig out my phone.

A bizarre call came over the walkies. "Has anyone spotted a stray sunbeam?"

I was growing weary of the secret language on this set. Oh, who was I kidding? I was tired of being the new kid who didn't fit in. I hated being an outsider.

A little girl, she couldn't have been more than three or four, appeared out of nowhere. She ran to the door of one office, sobbing. When she found it locked, she kicked it with her tiny sneakered foot and hurried to try the next one. The third one was my office, and that door was open. She threw open the door, ran inside, and slammed it shut behind her.

I couldn't stand the thought of any kid upset and alone like that. I pulled out my walkie. "If the sunbeam is wearing purple sparkles, she's in the director's office," I said.

"Ten-four. Will respond." Some faceless person answered.

I wasn't going to wait for someone else. I went to my office and made plenty of noise, rattling the handle before I opened the door and turned on the light. The little girl was nowhere to be seen, but the chair had been pushed back from the desk, and I thought I spotted a sparkly purple sneaker sticking out from underneath. I ignored the desk and sat on the couch instead. My guitar was there, propped against the arm. Desi had promised jam sessions, and I had come prepared. I strummed aimlessly at first, until the answer came to me. Kids liked animals. I didn't know any songs about puppies, but I knew "The Stray Cat Strut."

I heard her moving as soon as I hit the opening chords. By the time I sang about the black and orange cat, she peered over the top of the desk, curiosity piqued. I continued singing, never missing a flourish, but also carefully not acknowledging my audience of one until I played the final, rockabilly chord.

I finally got a good look at her. She had dark, glossy curls pulled into ponytails held by purple ribbons and big brown eyes with golden flecks that seemed awfully familiar. She wore a purple shirt that matched her shoes and bore the title "Master Builder" under multi colored LEGO bricks.

"Play it again," she said, bouncing and smiling. Whatever trauma had her in tears before was completely forgotten.

I complied because, frankly, she was too cute for words. She watched my fingers on the strings and swayed in place to the beat. Halfway through the bridge, Sami appeared in my doorway, and everything clicked into place. The girl was a small version of Sami, a relative, or could she be Sami's *daughter?* I nearly lost my place in the song, but managed to finish.

Sami cleared her throat.

"Mommy!" The little girl ran to Sami, leaving no doubt. "He plays guitar, isn't that cool?"

Sami knelt so they were eye to eye. "We talked about how important it is to stay where you're supposed to be. When you run away, everyone gets worried and we have to stop working to look for you."

The girl pouted. "But, Mommy..."

"But you were angry?" Sami asked gently. "Do you think that's a good reason to run away?" She didn't push much further, just scooped the little girl up and handed her off to an assistant. The girl appeared contrite, but her eyes still sparkled mischievously. I could tell she was a spirited little thing.

"I'll be there in a minute," Sami said.

The assistant carried the child away. She waved to me as they left. I waved back.

"Stay away from her," Sami said.

I ignored her anger. It wasn't really directed at me, anyway. "You have a daughter," I said. I knew I was grinning like a fool, but didn't care. This was a whole other side of Sami I never imagined existed.

"Does that make me suddenly unattractive? Good."

Normally it would. I didn't care much for kids. They were too much trouble to work with. I never considered them beyond that. This one though... "She's adorable. What's her name?"

"None of your business."

"That's a funny name." My charm rarely worked on Sami, but like a fool, I kept trying. "How did you keep her away from the press?"

"By surrounding myself with people I trust." Obviously, I was not included in that category.

"You're not secretly married, are you?"

She glared at me, and I relaxed. A child, but no partner. I still had hope.

"Thank you for..." she seemed at a loss. "Carmen loves music. Thank you for singing to her."

"She seems like a cool kid," I ventured. "Her mom is pretty cool too." I might not be interested in kids, but I had tremendous respect for single parents, having been mostly raised by one. I let my face show what I was thinking.

Sami studied me like I'd done something surprising. She'd looked at me that way once before, when Desi had been dealing with a personal crisis, and Sami came to the film set in support. Not for the first time, I wondered what she really thought of me. She smiled, a real one this time. Her hand landed on my arm, and just that casual contact sent a lightning through me. "Seriously, it's so scary when I can't find her. You have no idea... Just, thank you."

Chapter Eleven

JARROD

was accustomed to set schedules. Twelve hour days were pretty standard. I often worked longer on my sets. There was a lot to do, and sleep could be held off with caffeine. It was common for me to work on the task in front of me while my mind considered something else entirely. Usually, that was another part of the project I was working on or the next project. That afternoon, I kept thinking that a twelve hour day would feel that much longer for a child of... How old was Carmen? I hadn't asked. Wasn't that the first question for normal people? I knew nothing about kids. That would have been painfully obvious.

I found Sami in one of the extra offices and offered her a can of ginger ale.

"What's that?"

"I thought it was what you liked to drink," I said. It was what she'd had on that plane all those years ago.

"When I'm sick, maybe. Not every day."

"Oh." I sighed and looked at the can. "How old is Carmen?"

"She'll be four next month." Sami didn't even look up from the papers she was studying as she answered.

I did the math.

"You were pregnant when we met."

She looked at me then. I couldn't read her expression.

"You drank ginger ale on the plane and kept looking at the airsickness bag. I thought you were a nervous flyer."

"I'm surprised you noticed, given your aversion to people pitching their scripts," she said.

"I was an ass. You haven't let me forget that, no matter how many times I apologized, but you were pregnant. Is that why you backed out of the film?

Her eyes narrowed. "You honestly thought I would let one encounter with you affect my career?"

I gaped at her. "I felt bad about that, and you knew it. You let me feel guilty for *years*."

"If it changed the way you treated strangers who approached you, it was worth it," she said.

That hurt. My first instinct was to say something sharp in return, but Sami's body language didn't match her words. I'd sparred with her plenty of times. I'd seen her angry with Desi's ex-husband and dismissive of people like Graham Howard, a twit who had worked on Desi's film. This was neither of those things. An acting coach from my television days taught me to act with my whole body. She'd said shoulder position was as important as facial expressions. Sami's showed that she was feeling guilty, even if her words gave the opposite impression.

"This isn't you," I said. "This hard ass routine you go into every time you're around me is total bullshit, and we both know it. I've seen the way you talk to your fans. I can tell just being on this set for a day or more that you treat everyone from the intern fetching coffee to your creative partners like Mickey with the same level of respect." I laughed. I couldn't help it. Desi and Kass both said Sami didn't actually hate me. I'd never quite believed them until now. "I see *you*, Sam. So why don't we stop playing games?"

She blinked at me and swiftly looked away. Had I gone too far?

"Yes, I was pregnant when we met. I didn't know it yet. I'd just broken up with the guy. No big loss there."

I noticed she didn't call him her boyfriend.

She laughed without much humor. "The thing was, I'd been told I couldn't get pregnant. A fact he threw in my face when I told him about my... condition." She glanced at me and then away again. "He didn't want a baby, and I didn't think I'd get the chance again. I didn't need him. She was my child, not his."

She looked fierce when she said that, but there was pain underneath. I imagined what she must have gone through, the anger and the fear. Rejection hurt, even if it came from a guy who she didn't really want in her life, anyway. The prospect of raising a child alone was never an easy one.

"He's a fool," I said softly. Even in just the few minutes we'd spent together, I could tell Carmen was special, just like her mother.

Sami's lips twisted. "The doctor predicted a difficult pregnancy. I was on bed rest for most of it. My friends covered for me."

That explained how few episodes Sami had written in season two.

"So yeah, that's why I backed out of the film. Sorry, but the whole world doesn't revolve around you after all."

A call came over the walkies. It was time to get back to work. I stood, but leaned over the desk so Sami had to look up to meet my eyes. "You're beautiful when you pretend to be angry," I said, and left before she could reply.

Chapter Twelve

SAMI

ickey sat down next to me, almost quivering with anticipation. "Can we talk about it yet?"

I glanced around. "I should check on Carmen."

"Adriana is with her. She's home from college, so if you need someone..."

The tension between my shoulders eased a little. "Don't you ever get tired of saving my ass?"

Mickey grinned ruefully. "Nope. Never." We bumped fists.

"Okay, the funding is in. We need to set up a meeting. Before that, you and I need to go over the details. I had a fairly clear schedule for this week." I pursed my lips and took a deep breath before continuing. Jarrod was a nuisance on so many levels. "What do the next few days look like for you?"

Mickey wasn't a writer, but was incredible at technical details I found frustrating or tedious. We worked together so well because they excelled at things I didn't, and vice versa. We filled in each other's blanks. Kassi and Desi did that for me in the writers' room. I liked finding people who enjoyed doing things I didn't and setting them to those tasks. The difference being, Mickey didn't work for me. The

Rebel Light production company was a partnership in both our names.

Mickey's niece, Adriana, had Carmen engrossed in a game of Memory when I checked on them. "Great job! How did you get so smart? Let's try two more tiles this time. I'll use different pictures so we don't get mixed up."

Carmen saw me and beamed. "Mommy, I matched all the pictures. I'm really good at this!"

"That's great, baby," I said. "You two need anything?"

"No, we're okay," Carmen answered.

Adriana smiled at my daughter, then at me. "It's all good," she said. "Did Mickey tell you I'm home for a while? I'm free all week if you need me. "

"You're a life saver," I said.

"What color lifesaver?" Carmen asked.

"Green, of course," Adriana said. She had bright green stripes in her dark hair and wore green tights under black shorts that matched the green stripes on her black shirt. Mickey's family was large, loud, and everyone I'd met so far seemed to favor bold fashion choices. Mickey seemed almost conservative by comparison, favoring three piece bespoke suits, usually in typical business colors.

I'd been to several of their family functions over the years, enough to become an honorary member of the brood. I'd never been around people so accepting and supportive. I'd known Adriana since she was a teenager. She was Mickey's favorite relative. That was high praise.

"I'll try to finish early," I said.

"You're not staying for the j-a-m s-e-s-s-i-o-n?" she asked with a glance at Carmen.

"Not today," I said. Carmen would have enjoyed it, but I was exhausted already. Carmen began singing the alphabet song. Adriana joined in. I went back to my office. Why did everyone seem to relate to my daughter better than I did?

Jarrod caught me. "I know you're busy. I just have two questions." He wanted to verify the underlying conversation in a scene where the characters seemed to be discussing something else entirely. I was grudgingly impressed that he understood the subtext perfectly.

"That scene isn't on the schedule for today."

"I know. We have some extra time."

My next breath was tight. "What do you mean, extra time? The schedule is laid out so everything is..."

"And we're ahead of schedule. I asked everyone if they wanted to keep going, and they said yes."

In six seasons, we'd never once been ahead of schedule. We'd gotten better at being right on time instead of scrambling to catch up, but even that was a challenge some weeks. "You must have missed something," I said.

"I promise you, I didn't. Look, Sam, I know I'm the invader here, but I'll take care of your show. No one told me you were scheduled to direct when I signed on."

I didn't want to talk about that. My face should have told him as much, but he pressed on.

"I recognize this is your world and I shouldn't have stormed through the gates without permission."

Why did his metaphors all have double meanings? Or was that just my dirty mind at work? As much as I tried to ignore Jarrod with his devilishly handsome looks, even with all the problems I had to sort out, including my family issues, he always found a way into my thoughts.

"You said you had two questions?"

"Will you let me make it up to you?" His dark brown gaze suggested plenty of ways in which he could do that. I avoided looking at him directly.

"You did notice that I have a daughter, right?"

"Yes. Her name's Carmen, and she'll be four next month.

She's a little spitfire who likes music, though I don't know what kind yet."

"And you still want to make it up to me?"

His hand stopped just short of touching my face. "More than anything," he said. Intensity rolled off him in waves. He glanced around. "Tell me you never think about it. I can be done after this week if that's what you want. Just say it. Tell me it meant nothing to you."

Was that what I wanted? Jarrod and I had been playing this game for years. My pregnancy hadn't been an easy one. I spent many bleak days on bed rest, and worry filled my endless waking hours, concern for my career, concern for my pregnancy that was supposed to be impossible in the first place. Even then, Jarrod Colosi had been a bright spot. He'd been so certain I carried a grudge from that encounter on the plane that he sent random fruit bouquets, personalized M&M's and other silly gifts to my office. Every time my assistant appeared with a new offering, it made me smile. Jarrod had an annoying talent for sneaking around my defenses. I could have told him to leave me alone, but I just didn't want to.

My silence was an answer, just like it had been so many times before.

"Tell me to stop, and I will," he said.

The memory of the first time he'd said that washed over me. I saw it affecting him, too. "I'll let you know," I said finally.

His face lit up with a smile. It actually lit up, like there was a fire in him, and I made it burn brighter.

"Okay then." He said it with an upper Midwest accent.

I laughed. That was a set joke, spouting lines from *Fargo*, both the film and the series. Anyone who dared to say they were going to do something would get the response, "Okay, then." A chorus of people would then repeat the phrase, and even suggest to the first person, "Why don't you go do that then?" giving that first person the chance to say, "Okay then."

It had gone on for several minutes once, to everyone's amusement, except for a visiting producer who thought we were all ridiculous for wasting time. I found that time spent joking around was never truly wasted. Things like jam sessions and dance breaks wove the cast and crew into a tight unit, and that was the kind of place I wanted to work every day.

Adrianna agreed to watch Carmen for the rest of the week. I'd always liked Adrianna and was even more impressed by the young woman she'd become. She texted me a list of places she wanted to take Carmen in the afternoons before meeting up with me on the set. I'd had my share of babysitters through the years who were more interested in their phones than my child. There was a reason I didn't just call a service when Lucia left for her vacation. Adrianna was a refreshing change.

With Carmen squared away, I could focus on work, and my first concern was the schedule. I knew Jarrod liked to finish his projects early. He produced most of his films and had a reputation for coming in ahead of schedule and under budget. I figured he had to be cutting corners somewhere. If he was pushing my people too hard, I wanted to know about it.

But when I tried to enter the production office, it was locked. The editors worked their own schedules. Some were late risers and ambled onto set late morning, but worked well into the night. There were a few early birds, though. Damu was one of those. I knocked on the door and he answered.

"Hey, Sami."

"Good morning, Damu. Are you sure you're not sleeping here?" I teased.

He smiled. "There's less traffic at four in the morning."

"Four in the morning? That's when I look at the clock and am happy I have another two hours to sleep."

"That's what's so nice about it. Everyone else is asleep and I get the whole building to myself."

"Is there security footage of you streaking across the set?"

Damu laughed. "No, but Karla lost a bet once and…"

I stuck my fingers in my ears, "La, la, la, la," I sang. "I don't want to know."

Damu was still standing in the doorway, despite our comfortable conversation. That was odd. "Anyway," I said, "I wanted to get a look at the dailies from yesterday."

"Yeah, about that…" He shoved his hands into his pockets and scuffed his feet, avoiding my gaze.

"What about that? They got a lot done yesterday, supposedly."

"Oh, they did," he agreed, nodding. "We're way ahead of schedule."

My unease grew. "How far ahead of schedule?"

Damu shrugged.

"If they're rushing and cutting corners, I need to know about it."

"The dailies look really good, actually," he said.

"Wonderful. So let me see them."

"I can't." He stared at his feet again.

I took a deep breath to keep from raising my voice. "Damu, has there been some change that I'm unaware of? Did someone else become the show runner around here?" I never had to pull rank before.

Damu looked at me with wide eyes. "Oh no, nothing like that."

"Good. Glad to hear it. Now as show runner, I would like to look at the dailies."

"I'm not allowed to show them to anyone."

I inhaled through my nose and exhaled the same way,

while looking around to see if anyone was close enough to hear our conversation. Damu and Kassi ranked first and second for shyest people on set. It was anyone's guess which of the two would take the top spot. Point being, if I ripped Damu's head off in front of witnesses, he would run away and never come back. He was actually really good at his job, and I didn't want to lose him.

"Perhaps we have a misunderstanding," I said, fighting to keep my voice low and reasonable.

"Here comes Elena," Damu said. His shoulders didn't completely come down from around his ears, but they lowered an inch or two.

"G'morning, Sami," Elena said.

"Morning," I said. "Would you like to tell me what's going on here? Since when can't I see the dailies?"

"It's in the contract," Elena said. "The directors have a non-interference clause. Zuri doesn't use it, of course, and most of the guest directors don't know about it or don't care, but they can stipulate that only producers and editors see the dailies."

"And Jarrod is enforcing that clause," I said, fighting hard to keep my anger in check. This was one of the few episodes I wasn't producing because I had planned to direct it. Had he known that? So much for his acknowledgement that this world was mine and he had no business being in it. *That manipulative bastard*, I thought. Out loud, I said, "I understand you two are just the messengers here. Sorry to put you in this position."

Elena smiled, but Damu knew better. The tension didn't quite leave him. He fiddled with his long braids and scrubbed at the patch of hair on his chin. He watched me warily before disappearing into the production office with Elena. The lock clicked behind them. I gritted my teeth.

Waiting on my desk was a sad eyed Puss in Boots figurine

holding a purple rose. So Jarrod had been in my office. I wanted to smash the figurine and stomp on the flower, but Carmen liked all the Shrek characters, and she loved purple. I would give it to her. As for Jarrod, he was officially back on my shit list, and no number of silly gifts or flowers would get him off. No one got to waltz into my world and just take over. I'd been angry when he stole my finale. Now I was furious.

Chapter Thirteen

JARROD

I pushed the schedule as much as I could because that was how I operated. Extra time to play around or in case something went wrong, was always a good idea. This time, I had some shenanigans planned for the end of the week. Once I let everyone in on it, they were willing to work fast and take fewer breaks between scenes. The crew worked harder than anyone. To thank them, I supplied the food and drinks as well as participating in the evening jam sessions. The way to almost any group's heart was through their stomachs. Even Mickey warmed to me after the first night. For the last song of the jam session, we performed "Tempo" together. I did my best Missy Elliot impersonation. A few people had their phones out, but I didn't care if it ended up on the internet. There wasn't much left that could embarrass me.

Sami must have made arrangements for Carmen, because she wasn't on set after that first day. Sami seemed marginally more relaxed. On Tuesday, she wore a t-shirt that read, "Never judge a book by its movie." I agreed with that, so it was hardly an insult. I still had my assistant order a shirt for me via next day early a.m. delivery.

The next day, I wore a shirt with "Blame the writer" written on it in big block letters. Sami saw it and raised a single eyebrow in response. Her lips didn't even twitch. Desi laughed outright, but shut it down after a glance from her friend.

"I hate you," Sami said as she got close, not loud enough for anyone else to hear.

I leaned over to give my usual response, "No, you don't," and ended up getting a good whiff of her soap or conditioner or both. Jasmine and citrus went straight to my head. After that night we spent together, that scent had lingered on my sheets. I'd buried my face in them, trying to hold on to even that little bit of her.

My plan for working on *Death Sucks* had been to get Sami out of my system so I could move on and forget about her. Either we would get together and I'd realize that I'd been falsely enshrining that one night in my memory, or after a week, I'd see that we were completely incompatible like Sami claimed we were. Those were the only two outcomes I'd imagined. Finding more to admire about Samantha Augustine, the way she worked, the way she lived, hadn't been part of the bargain. How could I forget about her now? Of course, if she wanted me to leave, I would have. If I believed her at all when she muttered, "I hate you," I would have gone away and never troubled her again, but from Sami, "I hate you" meant something else entirely.

There were plenty of shenanigans on set, even as everyone worked faster than they ever had before. Desi shouted, "Dance break!" after we finished a take and swiped my lucky fedora right off my head. She must have planned this, because the music playing over the speakers was "One" from *A Chorus Line*. She was soon joined by actors, techs, and interns. They used everything from scripts to bowls as substitutes for hats, and they all seemed well versed in the steps.

I had played Zach, the director, for a while in the traveling production. It was easy to fall back into that role. "Desi, watch the other dancers!" I barked. She grinned. "Get your kicks in line." She made her dancing even more dramatic, defying my instructions. I laughed instead of shouting anything else.

The song finished and everyone went back to work. I held out my hand as Desi approached, but Sami appeared out of nowhere and snatched my hat out of Desi's hand. Sami placed it on her own head. Her expression dared me to say anything about it. She looked awfully sexy in my hat. I was tempted to let her keep it. She turned on her heel and strode into her office. I followed.

"Give me back my hat," I said, closing the door behind me.

"Give me back my show," Sami countered. She still had that dangerous light in her eyes.

"I'll be done on Friday. It will be all yours again."

"Good. You can have your hat back then. Maybe."

"Maybe." I scoffed. "You know, for some reason, I don't believe you."

"So you, what? Require a guarantee? Some sort of proof?"

I fought a smile. "Yeah, something like that." She wouldn't rise to my challenge. Plenty of experience told me that, but then she dropped the hat on a table, crossed the space between us and pulled my face down to hers.

Sami's lips were just as I remembered them, soft and sensual, though not exactly yielding. She took as much as she gave. It was always like that between us, a struggle for control. I fucking loved it. She gripped my hair in her fists and ran her tongue along mine. I had just let my hands settle on her waist when she backed away, leaving me breathless.

Her face still held that challenge. *I dare you*, her expression said. She grabbed my hat and walked out the door while I waited for blood to circulate to my brain again.

The day progressed, and I did my best to concentrate. Without my hat, I tended to rake my fingers through my hair – a lot. It was a nervous habit I had picked up when I started working behind the camera, and one that I had thought was broken. Apparently, it had only been dormant. The state of my nerves, or just my hair, seemed to strike a chord on set. I saw a lot of suppressed grins and shoulders shaking with silent laughter. And just like that, I was the substitute teacher again.

I escaped to my office during a break. Sami's office had been empty. The writers' room was my next stop. I wanted my hat back, dammit.

A small wooden box sat in the center of my desk. The only clue was a purple sticky note with my name on it written in Sami's familiar scrawl. I lifted the lid. Inside was a pile of dirt, no, ashes, and on top of that rested the feather from my fedora.

A bolt of shock, followed quickly by fury, shot through me. She burned my hat? My *lucky* hat? I replayed the events of the morning, my "Blame the Writer" shirt, countered with the rose and cat figurine, the silliness on set and Desi stealing my hat. They had planned this. But Sami had kissed me. That damn kiss curled my toes and threw me off more than not having my hat. That was her plan, I realized. She wanted to throw me off. She had all but accused me of being a spoiled brat who always got his way. I took a deep breath and unclenched my fists. She was trying to get under my skin. She'd done it for sure this time, but I couldn't let her know.

It hurt. I'd had that hat for years, almost since I started directing. Destroying it was mean, and lower than we'd ever gone before. It made the way she'd kissed me manipulative instead of... What had I hoped for? That it was real? That she relived the night we spent together as often as I did? I shook my head. Obviously, that wasn't the case.

Kass was passing by as I left my office. She jerked her head up and startled a little when she saw me. This was nothing new. Kassi spent a lot of time lost in her thoughts. It was probably the secret to being such a prolific writer. She always seemed to be working something out in her mind. When she was present, she saw everything. I'd learned all this when we worked together on her film.

"Jarrod? What's wrong?" she asked.

"Ask your best buddy," I said. It came out harsher than intended.

Kassi actually backed up a step.

"I guess you weren't in on it then," I said.

"In on what?"

I held out the box. She opened it and her eyes went wide. I watched her expression change from shock to anger. Her dark eyebrows drew down. Kassi didn't like teasing, even when she wasn't the object of it. She was also a fierce defender of her friends. I didn't think I qualified, but what she did next changed my mind.

"You know how we won all those awards this year?" she asked.

"Of course," I said. I'd been at all the ceremonies. Kassi actually hadn't gone to any of them.

"We have them in a cabinet near the writers' room. Sami thought it would be fun to keep them there where everyone could see."

Kass said that like her words had a deeper meaning. I tried, but I wasn't getting it. She was much smarter than I was.

"It's a trophy cabinet," Kassi said, emphasis on every word. "For trophies. Things that you win in a competition."

Realization finally dawned. Relief swept through me. "Thanks, Kass," I said.

I left the box in my office and all but ran to the writers' room. I had seen the case before. There, balanced on the Golden Globe, was my fedora. The feathers were intact, which meant Sami had gone through the trouble of finding lookalikes. It was a good prank. I had to admit that much, even if I didn't appreciate being the butt of the joke.

I looked around and found a surprising number of people conveniently in the area. "Does anyone have a key to this thing?" I asked to general laughter.

"It's not locked!"

Of course it wasn't. Everyone was family on this set. They could be trusted. I caught sight of Sami watching from the door of the writers' room as I retrieved my hat and closed the glass case. She turned away and disappeared into the room. I held my hat up like a prize to applause and laughter.

"We're back in five," I reminded everyone and followed Sami into the room.

The room was exactly what I expected. A long conference table surrounded by plush chairs took up the center. The walls alternated credenzas and couches. Glass apothecary jars sat atop the credenzas. They held candy of varying color and types. I spotted one with Sami's cherry lollipops. The walls were covered with whiteboards and monitors, except for one wall which held promotional posters for *Death Sucks, Under the Water* and *Error of the Moon*. I couldn't help smiling. It was a cool room. I could feel creativity crackling in the air like a static charge.

Sami was watching me, I realized. She didn't seem amused.

"So this is where the magic happens," I said, because I had to say something to break the silence.

"Is that the best you could manage?" she asked and added, "Lame."

"Okay, so I'm lame," I said. "And you're not nice. At least we know where we stand."

"Oh, am I 'not nice'?" she said, letting her lower lip stick out and giving me sad eyes. "Poor baby. You shouldn't expect everyone to kiss your ass all the time."

I didn't appreciate the mockery. It made my teeth grind. I also wanted to draw that pouty lip into my mouth. Her lips tasted sweet, like those cherry lollipops. Wanting her despite the way she'd manipulated me made my jaw ache.

"How did you feel when you thought I'd destroyed something you cared about? Were you upset? Angry? Did you take it personally, Jarrod?" She was still using that condescending voice.

She hadn't talked to Carmen that way. No, I was getting the special treatment. She was calling me a spoiled child. That message came through loud and clear. She stepped close to me, coming in for the kill. I gripped my hat tighter.

"How do you think this week has made me feel?" she asked, not in her regular voice, but low and dangerous. Her eyes flashed like a big cat in the zoo that would rip my throat out if not for the protective glass keeping us apart.

Her glare cut through me, but I refused to let that show. I wanted to back away from her anger, but I didn't do that either. Instead, I leaned closer so our noses almost touched. "That's the difference between us, Sam. I would never even consider destroying something you loved."

I turned and left before she came up with a response that would no doubt cut me to ribbons. I'd been feeling a little guilty about my plan for Friday. Now I had no regrets.

A young woman in full punk gear, from her black Doc Martens to her green and black striped hair, brought Carmen to the set as we were finishing for the day.

"Hi, Jarrod!" Carmen said. She shared her mother's propensity for fandom t-shirts. This one featured Keira Knightley in full pirate regalia and the words, "Elizabeth Swann, Pirate King" scrawled above and below.

I knelt down to Carmen's level. "Hey, sweet pea, it's nice to see you again."

"Will you sing for me?"

"I sure will." I scooped her up and dropped my hat on her head. "Oh, sweet pea..." She giggled and wrapped her arms around my neck. "Dance with me," I sang as we danced in a small circle. Her cheek pressed against mine. "Oh, sweet pea..." It was an old song, older than I was, but one of the scenery guys knew it and joined in. He danced with the punk girl. She laughed and twirled in her boots.

I spun in a circle, and Carmen hid her face in my shoulder. My hat fell to the ground. Sami watched from the side. A few others looked on. They were smiling. Sami was not.

I set Carmen down and retrieved my hat. Sami and I weren't on the best terms at the moment, but did she really want me to stay away from her daughter? Why? I couldn't understand that any more than I understood my impulse to entertain the little girl. Carmen had charmed me in the space of a few minutes. I'd heard men talk about being wrapped around their daughter's little finger before, but it hadn't made sense until now.

Whoa. *Daughter?* Where had that come from? I didn't want to be a father, and Sami certainly wouldn't want me auditioning for the job. Desi appeared and got Sami walking away as they talked. Carmen looked back at me over her mother's shoulder and waved. I waved back.

That kid's smile could melt an ogre's heart. I didn't stand a chance. They were dangerous, the pair of them, but the whole home and family scene wasn't for me. I hurried back to where the crew was working to set up for the next day. Soon they would eat, and then the music would start. This was my life. I could spend long hours on set because nothing waited for me but a large, empty house. There might be a car in the garage that I tinkered with in my spare time, but even there, I was between projects. My next script, a huge blockbuster featuring lots of car chases and explosions, waited for me. I hadn't looked at it yet. It wasn't that I only focused on one project at a time. No one could accuse me of that. I just hadn't looked at the script since I first signed on to the project. After I was done here, then I could focus on other things. I *would* focus on things that didn't include Samantha Augustine. Huge action sequences and car chases could be a nightmare, but they ought to keep me busy for a while.

Chapter Fourteen

SAMI

I walked onto the set Friday morning with my coffee in one hand and my messenger bag over my shoulder.

Calls of "Morning, Sami!" and "Hey, Sami," greeted me.

"Good morning. Happy Friday!" I did a little dance. No one joined in. "Why doesn't anyone ever dance with me?" I asked, but got no answer.

Cameraman Pete stood to the side in a mobile rig and his first assistant, Aiden, behind him.

"Hey, Pete," I called. He backed up as if he was keeping me in frame. Aiden made sure no one and nothing was in the way.

"Are you filming me? Stop it. That's weird." I held my travel mug in front of my face. He didn't stop. "This is very exciting," I said. "Me going into my office. Be sure to record that for posterity. Bye now."

The door was just slightly ajar. I hesitated and looked back at Pete, who was now shooting over my shoulder. They were up to something. The door opened, seemingly of its own accord, and inside, lit from the floor in that creepy way that elongated his face, stood the murderous zombie clown Chuckles.

"Oh, fuck me!" I cried.

It was Jarrod. I knew it was Jarrod. But in the costume and makeup, I couldn't actually *see* that it was Jarrod. The movie had come out shortly after I graduated college. It terrified me. Clowns were probably my least favorite characters in anything, and the gruesome gash on his face, showing gristle of tendons and bone, didn't help matters at all.

"I'll dance with you, Sami," he said in that creepy, hoarse voice.

"Nope, nope, and nope," I said, backing away. "Jarrod, stop it."

He took a step toward me.

"I'm serious, Jarrod. Stop it now."

"Who's Jarrod? I'm Chuckles the clown. Don't you want to dance with me, Sami?"

I dropped my bag, turned, and hurried away. I could hear his footfalls behind me. The whole camera crew was in on the joke, because I passed two others filming me. I wasn't quite running, but it was close. I tried to find an office where I could escape, but of course, most of them were locked. It was our last day filming for the season. Work would continue for the producers and editing department, but many others had left the set already.

The conference room wasn't locked. I jerked the door open, intending to run inside and slam it shut behind me before Jarrod could catch up. I could sit in there all damn day if I had to.

The lights came on and the crowd within shouted, "Surprise!" They burst into an up tempo rendition of "Happy Birthday."

"We ordered you a clown," Mickey said.

A white gloved hand tapped my shoulder. I refused to

turn. Jarrod reached around with his other hand and held up a candied apple.

"Want some candy?"

"Get the fuck away from me," I said to laughter from everyone else.

There was a full breakfast buffet waiting for us, including a chef who would make omelets or anything else on request. It was quite nice, or would have been if a certain creepy clown wasn't hovering just at the corner of my peripheral vision.

"The network wanted to show their appreciation," Mickey said.

"That's nice," I said, smiling a little tightly. No one from the network was in attendance, I noticed. It was better that way. We could all relax and enjoy ourselves. The show was up for renewal in a year. Those talks would begin soon enough.

"They want to know what direction the next season will take," Mickey said.

"I'll let them know as soon as I do," I said. I had a vague idea, but with the end of the contracts looming, there was always the chance that we wouldn't get renewed, and then we would owe it to the fans to wrap things up and provide closure. The added complication of Mickey and I working on another series, limited though it was, in Germany, probably wouldn't help in the negotiations. I glanced around the room at all the people who depended on me for their livelihoods.

Mickey, meanwhile, looked at something just past my shoulder.

"He's right behind me, isn't he?"

Mickey nodded.

"I'm going to ignore him until he goes away."

Mickey nodded again, but our conversation turned stilted as we tried to make small talk. Neither of us excelled at that. I didn't know what Jarrod was doing behind me, but Mickey suppressed a laugh more than once. I went to the other side of the room, where members of the makeup department clustered. "Really, you guys?" I teased. "Traitors."

"It was fun," Sue Li confessed.

"I bet."

"One of my mentors worked on the first film," Obi said. "She sent me her notes."

"I guess the costume is on loan?" I asked.

They nodded.

Desi joined us, but kept looking just above and behind me.

"Is he still there?"

"Yup." She tried not to laugh, but wasn't very successful.

I shook my head and got in line to order an omelet. Jarrod followed. I could tell that by the way people watched me. I ignored him and them, got my omelet and chose a table. Kassi joined me. I had the feeling it was for moral support. Desi was off being social with the props department.

Jarrod leaned over and took my left wrist in his gloved hands. I ignored him. He did something. I couldn't tell what since I refused to look, and placed my hand back on the table, giving it a little pat as he did. I felt a tug and looked at my hand. A ribbon was looped and tied around my wrist. It led to a spotted balloon. Chuckles the Clown had a liking for polka dots. They were one of his signatures. I jerked at the ribbon. "Get it off!" It took a moment for me to calm down enough to undo the knot and let the evil thing float to the ceiling.

Everyone laughed. I sighed, looking heavenward, and turned to Jarrod. His dark eyes danced. They were the only part of him that I recognized. "You're not going to stop, are you?"

"Why would I stop, Sami? I want you to come back to the circus with me. Then we can play together forever and ever…"

"Ahhh! Stop it!" I said with a shudder. I turned to Kassi. "How do we end this?"

She thought for a moment. A smile spread across her face. I knew that smile. It meant she had an idea, probably a brilliant one. "Zuri!" she called to our regular director.

Zuri came over. "What's up?" She giggled a little at Jarrod and my obvious discomfort.

"I have a way to end it."

"Oh, we're doing an ending?" Zuri said.

"You didn't plan an ending?" I asked.

"No, we were just going to film the initial appearance and the surprise party. I think Pete has been getting some more footage between bacon and egg sandwiches, but there wasn't a real plan or anything." Zuri said.

And that was why we were the writers.

"I've got an ending," Kassi said. "I'll get with editing later and we'll piece it all together to show at the wrap party. It will be perfect."

Of that, I had no doubt.

Apparently, I was the only person who came in with the actual intention of working. Everyone else knew it was a day long prelude to the wrap party. There was an area clear for a jam session and dancing, not terribly unusual for us, but still a surprise to me.

"Just how far ahead of schedule were you?" I asked Jarrod.

He shrugged and did a little dance, still in full character. His dark eyes sparkled with mischief.

"How long have you been planning this?" Costumes didn't get loaned out on a day's notice. This all could have been revenge for my hat prank, but I didn't think so.

"Oh, Sami," he said in that creepy voice. "I've been watching you for a long time. I've wanted you to come play with me…"

I held up a hand. "Forget it. I'm sorry I asked." I was going to have nightmares if this didn't end soon.

"Okay," Kassi said to me. "We spotlight Jarrod in the middle of the floor, play 'Everybody Loves a Clown' 'Tears of a Clown' or 'Clown Strike', something like that. You say a line to the camera, something like, 'this won't end until I dance with him, will it?' and then, dragging your feet, go dance with Jarrod, who is standing with his arms out in invitation."

"Then what?" I asked. I'd done summer stock in college, but I knew my limitations. Acting was not on my list of skills. I belonged behind the cameras, not in front.

"You dance for a few beats. He spins you around and breaks your neck."

"I die?"

"Oh yeah."

"I love it," Zuri said.

"Me too," Jarrod agreed in that creepy voice.

"Nobody asked you," I snapped without much venom.

"Then the camera zooms in on Jarrod's face and he does that creepy laugh, and cut!" Kassi beamed.

"We'd better try it a few times," Zuri said.

I gave them all a look, but had to admit, it was a good ending.

It took more than a few practice runs. The problem wasn't the line. That was easy. I could show plenty of trepidation in my walk, too. Truth be told, being around him for hours had done nothing to make me comfortable with Jarrod in that creepy costume. We swayed together, and I let him spin me.

"You're turning your head," Zuri directed. "Like you're anticipating what he's going to do. Try not to do that."

"Do you trust me?" Jarrod asked.

"In that get up?" I said. "No way."

Laughter behind me. Oh great, we had an audience. Pete

was filming all of this. I could imagine what he'd do with it later. The editing room was in for a good laugh.

"Just look straight ahead," Jarrod said. "Let me turn your head. They can speed it up in post-production if necessary."

"Fix it in post!" the shout came.

Jarrod smiled. He had a permanent leering grin painted on his face, but his lips actually turned up this time. "Just remember to look scared and drop on cue. I'll do the rest."

"Like I have to remember to look scared," I said.

He studied me. One gloved hand rose, but stopped before it reached my face. "I'd never..."

"Quiet," I hissed. Pete was right over my shoulder, no doubt getting this entire exchange.

Jarrod nodded. "Shall we give it a try?" he asked, then ducked his head to Zuri. "Sorry. It's a habit."

She grinned. "No problem. You ready, Sami?"

I took my place. The music began, playing low. They would overdub it at regular volume later. Everyone in the dance area moved to it. Everyone but Chuckles the creepy zombie clown, of course.

"I have to dance with him, don't I?" I asked Pete. He moved the camera up and down in the affirmative.

I sighed audibly. Another camera was already focused on Jarrod, where he stood with his hand extended toward me. Pete stayed on me as I walked slowly, full of dread, and took Jarrod's hand. We danced for a few lines while Smokey Robinson sang. Jarrod twirled me during the instrumental part and jerked me back, mid twirl, against his chest. I gave the camera wide eyes as Jarrod caught my chin with one hand and pulled it to the left. That was my cue to drop. I didn't fall completely, just out of the shot. My heart pounded. Most of me knew it was just pretend, but some part of me wasn't so sure. Or maybe it was being close to Jarrod like that. My body remembered and responded to the roughness, play acting or not, as it had before.

"Perfection!" Zuri called. "Print it." She beamed.

Jarrod offered me a hand up. I took Kassi's instead. "Creepy motherfucker," I muttered to her and to Pete behind the camera. He hadn't stopped recording yet.

Kassi went into the editing room to help with the final cut. I turned to Jarrod. "Are you going to take that shit off?"

"Why would I do that, Sami?" he asked.

"You really need to stop that," I said. But anything else I had intended to say died on my tongue.

"Mommy!" Carmen ran over to me. "I made you something for your birthday, but it's at home." She looked up at the clown. "Hi, Jarrod! We're going to have cake for Mommy's birthday, wanna come?"

I studied my daughter. "How did you know that was Jarrod?" It would have been a good idea to warn Carmen about the zombie clown so she wouldn't be scared, but I'd seen Adrianna's face when they came into the room. She'd been expecting the usual people on set, not a creepy clown.

"I just know," Carmen answered with a shrug. She regarded Jarrod. "Your face is all messy, silly clown."

"I'm a zombie too," Jarrod said. He'd dropped his Chuckles persona for Carmen. I would have appreciated a little of that consideration.

"Do you eat brains?" Carmen asked. We'd watched the original *Night of the Living Dead*. Carmen and Mia spent the next week pretending to be zombies in search of brains. To them, any monster movie filmed in black and white was more humorous than scary.

Jarrod nodded, moaned like those old time zombies and stretched his arms out straight.

"That's yucky. Cauliflower looks like brains. I bet it tastes like them too."

Jarrod laughed. I sighed. Vegetables and my daughter did not get along.

"Do you like mashed potatoes?" he asked her.

Carmen nodded.

"I know how to make cauliflower taste like mashed potatoes."

"No way!" Carmen said.

"Yes way!" Jarrod replied. "I'll-" He glanced at me. His smile faded a bit. It showed even through the greasepaint. "I'll tell your mommy how to cook them. How would that be?"

"Okay," Carmen said.

"Okay." Jarrod agreed.

"Mommy, can Jarrod have cake with us?"

I didn't know what to say. Carmen had adults that came in and out of her life all the time. She understood when I told her an actor we knew was working on the other side of the world. We found the countries on the globe and read about them on the internet. So why did I worry about her getting attached to Jarrod? He would be gone soon, off filming his next project somewhere, and we would go on without him. Why did that thought make my stomach twist?

"I have lots of work to do tonight, sweet pea," Jarrod said. "And I have to get this makeup off. That takes a long time."

"Just use makeup remover, silly," Carmen said. She had visited the makeup department on Monday and learned all sorts of new things.

"This is a different kind of makeup. Want to see?" He leaned in. I was surprised that he didn't converse with Carmen the way most people spoke to children. There was nothing condescending in Jarrod's manner. He indulged her curiosity and even encouraged it.

Carmen dragged one finger down his cheek. It came away

white with grease paint. She rubbed her finger and thumb together, smearing the makeup. "It's sticky."

I pulled a tissue out of my pocket and cleaned her fingers before the greasepaint ended up on her clothes or mine. "Maybe Jarrod can come to the wrap party tomorrow night," I said.

"I didn't know I was invited," Jarrod said, his usual cocky tone strangely absent. My hat prank had turned out darker than I'd intended. Or maybe I had meant it that way. I wasn't sure anymore.

"I invite you," Carmen said. "Bring your guitar, okay?"

"And ditch the clown costume," I added. So what if he came to the party? There would be lots of people around. What was the worst that could happen?

PART TWO

"Layla"

Chapter Fifteen

JARROD

I arrived fashionably late to Sami's house the next night. Town cars lined the circular driveway. A group of drivers relaxed on the wide covered terrace with their own buffet, extra-large cooler, and a television. Of course, Sami would employ drivers to make sure everyone got home safely, and of course, she would make sure those drivers were comfortable while they waited.

I didn't recognize the person who opened the door, but spotted Desi at a baby grand piano with Carmen at her side. Desi played the "Habanera" from *Carmen*.

"Sing it!" Carmen insisted.

"It's French," Desi said. "You wouldn't understand a word."

"Sing the one from the movie," Carmen insisted.

"You let her watch *Carmen Jones?*"

Desi smiled over her shoulder at me. "It is my responsibility as an Auntie to be a corrupting influence. We turned it off before the end."

"Hi, Jarrod!" Carmen said. She spotted the sparkly purple bag in my hand. "Is that for me?"

"Perhaps," I said. She all but bounced with excitement. I knelt so I would be on her level. "If the recipient of this present you would be, you must answer questions three."

Carmen giggled. "Okay."

Desi stopped playing and turned to watch.

"Who played Carmen Jones in that movie you watched?"

Carmen looked at Desi and whispered the answer. Desi nodded. I pretended not to notice. "Dorothy Dandridge," Carmen said. "She was pretty. I like the guy in the movie too. He was on *The Muppet Show*."

I raised one eyebrow at Desi, who smiled and shrugged. So that was her influence, too.

"Harry Belafonte," I said.

"Yeah, him. He sings, 'Day-o!'"

"Oh, boy," Desi groaned softly.

"You like *The Muppet Show*?" I asked.

Carmen nodded enthusiastically.

"I have two favorite songs from the Muppets. Maybe you can guess one. I'll give you a hint. Pink cows sing it."

Her face brightened instantly. "Munah Munah!" she danced around singing it.

"Sami will not thank you for that," Desi said, but filled in the "doo doo doo doo" parts. "Last time, she sang it for two weeks straight."

"One more question," I said, interrupting the song. Carmen suddenly remembered the present and waited expectantly. This would be an impossible question for most kids, but I trusted Desi's influence. "Name the four Beatles."

Carmen rolled her brown eyes in a way very reminiscent of her mother. "John, Paul, George and Ringo," she answered without hesitation.

I handed her the bag. She grinned.

"Hey, manners," Desi said.

"Thank you, Jarrod." Carmen wrapped one arm around my neck and planted a kiss on my cheek.

"You're welcome, sweetie. I hope you like it."

"I will," she answered and ran off happily. "Mommy, look!"

"I see," Sami said. "Why don't you open it in your room so nothing gets lost or trampled?" She gave me one raised eyebrow. "Are you trying to bribe my daughter?"

I got to my feet. "Of course not." I held out a wine gift bag. "You, on the other hand..."

"Have fun with that," Desi said and promptly made herself scarce.

Sami peered at the bottle. It was a Spanish red that promised black cherry, plum, and cocoa notes. "Let me guess, you think we should share this over dinner?"

"Nope," I said lightly. "That one's just for you. We'll have something else with dinner."

"You have this all planned out, don't you?"

I shrugged and leaned in close enough to catch her perfume. It went straight to my head every time. "That's what I do," I breathed into her ear. Goosebumps rose on her neck and god, I wanted to trail my tongue through them, but I just gave her my best cocky grin, picked up my guitar and went out on the deck where Desi had promised there would be music.

Chapter Sixteen

SAMI

I had spent most of the day preparing for the party. Adrianna was busy all weekend, so I also had to keep track of Carmen while overseeing all the other details. I'd had a headache since breakfast, and the ibuprofen only barely kept it at bay. The caterers knew how to do their jobs, and I knew enough to stay out of their way. So I greeted my guests and tried to keep an eye on Carmen, who ran from group to group, soaking up the attention everyone was happy to give her.

Laughter and cheers from drinking games drifted up from the patio. I knew Kassi would be some place quieter, probably by the fire pit. So she was fine. Desi was part of the impromptu jam session on the deck. That was perfectly normal. I could pick out Jarrod's voice, too, which was why I was avoiding the deck. We were a musically inclined group. There was no denying that. Normally, I would be right out there with them. The truth was, something in me melted when Jarrod sang. He was too handsome already. Put a guitar in his hands, or worse, put him on a stage with a guitar, and I was as lost as any rock band groupie, not that I would ever admit that out loud.

As it was, I was tempted to join Kassi. A sore throat had joined my headache. I requested a frozen margarita from the bar. My grandfather's prescription for most illnesses was a shot of tequila and bed rest. That option was not open to me, but the frozen drink soothed my throat. I made sure the bartender only put in half a shot of tequila. The caterers had taken over my kitchen. It seemed like a good time to make sure they had everything they needed and authorize their payment. Was I avoiding my own party? Of course not.

It occurred to me that I hadn't seen Carmen in a while. Normally, I sent her to Lucia's if I was having a party. A child didn't need to be around the raucous drinking that happened at these sorts of events. But with Lucia still M.I.A., I didn't really have a choice. I found Carmen exactly where I expected. She was always drawn to music like a bee to a flower, all the better if she could climb up on Desi's lap and be in the center of it all. I left her there long past her normal bedtime. I didn't feel like arguing with her, and I didn't feel like engaging in any conversations with my guests. It was easier to sit off to the side in the dark where no one would notice me.

I needed a break, just a few days, but I had no down time in sight. Proposals for the new show were due, and I had to meet with my writers on the other shows to discuss upcoming seasons. I'd planned this schedule specifically because I liked going from one project to the next. I used to get antsy and irritable when I wasn't working on something. Now, I wanted nothing more than a few days of doing nothing.

"Are you hiding?" Kassi asked. "That's my thing, you know. No copycats allowed."

"You sound like Carmen," I said.

"Where is the munchkin, anyway?"

"With her other auntie and all the guitars. That kid is going to run away to follow a band across the country, I just know it."

"If Desi has anything to do with it, Carmen will be fronting her own band. She won't be chasing after anyone."

I liked that idea better. "Are you heading out?"

"Yeah, I've done enough socializing for a month or two. Theo will be here in a minute."

"You could have brought him," I said.

"I am capable of doing things on my own, you know." Kassi smiled ruefully. "Besides, he likes parties as much as I do."

"Oliver's still in Atlanta?"

"He'll be home tomorrow afternoon." Her smile grew broader. *Home*. She'd never had a real home before. It still boggled my mind that Kassi, our Kassi, who ran away whenever anyone said boo, would find happiness with not one man but two. Then again, I saw the way they took care of her, and maybe that made up for what she had been missing her whole life. Kassi was happier than I'd ever seen her. She had a peace and a confidence she'd never had before. She deserved her two men and anything else it took to achieve that. I would personally make sure the tabloids left her alone, if that's what it took.

"What?" she asked.

I shook my head. "The Vikings are good for you."

She rolled her eyes. "Yeah, I might keep them."

"Might." I scoffed. "If you think they are ever letting you go again, you're crazy. Let's go find my daughter. She should be in bed."

Kassi was enough to draw Carmen away from the guitar circle. I doubted I could have done it on my own. To my daughter, apparently, every adult she encountered was more fun than me. We walked to the door together. Theo was just getting out of his car. He was tall, lean, and entirely too pretty for someone who shied away from the spotlight. The camera would love him if only he would get in front of one. He was polite enough with me, but his real warmth came out for Carmen. Theo caught her as she ran to him and lifted her high up onto his shoulder. I wondered if Kassi had considered having children with her men. Theo had dad material written all over him. He and Carmen conversed easily about some animated series I had never heard of, until Kassi put her hand on his arm and nodded to me.

"See you soon, *flicka*," Theo said, setting Carmen down at my side. He smiled at me and took Kassi's hand.

"We should have dinner," I said. "All of us."

"*All* of us?" Kassi asked with a wicked grin.

I rolled my eyes. "On the other hand..."

"Ollie bought a grill," Theo said. "Well, it started as a grill and turned into an outdoor kitchen. It'll be done once my pizza oven finally arrives. We could get together at our house."

They would want to be somewhere the paparazzi wouldn't follow. A private space was a good idea. "I'd like that." I said. "We'll have to coordinate schedules."

"We'll definitely try," Kassi said. Her expression said the gathering would probably end up being a while in the future. I didn't like that. Kassi, Desi and I had been tight since college. We'd never had trouble scheduling a ladies' night or weekend getaway before. But Desi was headed to Ireland and Kassi would be wrapped up in Oliver for an indeterminate amount of time after being apart. I fought the familiar sinking feeling in my stomach. Everyone let me down eventually. I didn't want to think that about my best friends. It was better to blame the men for complicating everything.

I watched the car turn out onto the street. "Time for you to go to bed," I told my daughter.

"No!" was her immediate reaction.

"Carmen Maria, it is almost eleven o'clock. You should have been asleep hours ago." I closed the front door behind us.

Carmen burst into tears and tore her hand from mine. She ran away before I could catch her again. My head throbbed harder.

Chapter Seventeen

JARROD

I left the deck and headed inside. Sami's house was of Craftsman style, though larger than any I'd seen before. The décor was tasteful and warm, but didn't showcase her personality much. People filled the deck, patio, and the main rooms. I'd barely seen Sami at all. Was she avoiding me?

Carmen pushed through a cluster of people. Tears streamed down her face. I stepped into her path. She crashed into me. I caught her and picked her up. "What's wrong, sweet pea?"

She sobbed an answer, but I couldn't understand anything but "bed." That was enough. What else would have a little kid so upset? "Oh, I see. Your mommy wants you to go to bed?"

Carmen nodded and rubbed at her eyes. She was tired. Anyone could see that, but she also had a stubborn streak to match her mother's. I spotted Sami across the room. She looked tired too, with a healthy dose of parental exasperation on top of it. I pointed to Carmen, still crying into my shoulder, held up one hand and mouthed "Five minutes?"

Sami scowled and threw up her hands. "Whatever." I

didn't need to read her lips. I heard her even in the populated space. She walked into the kitchen. I'd worry about her later.

"Tell you what," I said to Carmen. "What if we sing a song and I tell you a story? Will that make this whole bedtime situation a little more acceptable to you?"

She pouted, but nodded. She really was tired, the poor little kid. The living room was too crowded. I had spotted a den earlier. Still carrying Carmen, I went back onto the deck to retrieve my guitar and turned off all but one light in the den. This was where they actually lived. It was clean, but a toy box stood in the corner, and there were scuff marks on the table. The sectional showed signs of actual use, unlike the one in the formal living room. I liked this room a lot better.

"You sit here," I said, setting Carmen on the couch. "Did you ever figure out what my other favorite Muppet song was?"

Carmen shook her head, but she recognized the song as soon as I started to play and brightened right up. She even sang along. What a sweetie.

"Don't forget my story," she said when I'd finished.

I set my guitar aside. "Okay, once upon a time, there was a pirate warrior princess named..."

"Carmen!"

"Carmen, of course, because that is what all pirate warrior princesses should be named."

She grinned and shifted so she could snuggle under my arm. I'd never been one for kids, but damn if this one didn't make my heart melt.

"One night, Carmen's mother, the pirate warrior queen, threw a great party. There was music and lots of food, but eventually, it was time for princesses to go to bed."

"I'm not a princess. I'm a pirate," Carmen insisted.

"You're a pirate warrior princess," I corrected. "There's no rule against being all three. Anyway, Carmen had a secret that even her Mommy didn't know."

"What?" she asked.

"Carmen's bedroom was magical. If, when she went to bed, she lay very still and counted to..." I paused. "Can you count to one hundred?"

She nodded.

"If she lay very still and counted to one hundred, her bed would turn into a pirate ship and she could go on adventures. So, when the pirate queen said it was time for bed, Carmen brushed her teeth, in case she met any Kraken in her adventures."

"Kraken?"

"Of course. Kraken simply cannot tolerate minty fresh breath. It is known." I nodded solemnly. "Why do you think Captain Jack got taken to Davy Jones' locker? He never brushed his teeth." I knew she'd watched those films and was willing to bet they had started her pirate phase. "Everyone knows Captain Jack has stinky breath."

Carmen nodded agreement

"So, after Carmen brushed her teeth, and her mommy tucked her into bed, she lay very still and started to count. When she got to fifty, she could smell the ocean air. When she got to sixty, she felt her hair move in the wind. By seventy, her bed rocked like the deck of a ship. So every night, Carmen had wonderful adventures, and she told her mommy about them the next day over breakfast. The pirate queen thought Carmen was talking about her dreams, but Carmen knew that it was real. It was her magical secret. The end."

Carmen smiled up at me.

"Was that a good story?"

She nodded.

I heard a sound behind me. "Is that your mommy?" I asked.

Carmen nodded again.

"Is she mad?"

Carmen shook her head. I whistled and wiped my forehead. Carmen tried to suppress her grin.

"Let's go," Sami said.

This time, Carmen went without argument, though she came running back. "Thank you, Jarrod."

"You're welcome, sweet pea."

"Good night."

"Good night. Sweet dreams."

Chapter Eighteen

SAMI

I wanted to lie down and go to sleep right next to Carmen. Maybe I was dehydrated. I had that dizzy, disconnected feeling. My head pounded in time with my heartbeat. I had to pin on a happy face for my guests. Past parties had gone almost until dawn. I hoped that wouldn't be the case tonight.

Jarrod was in my kitchen, chatting up the caterers. Of course, he could charm everyone he met. Mr. Wonderful there had even charmed my daughter into a quiet, relaxing bedtime. How could he do that when, for me, it was a fight every damn time? I got some water and didn't hide my glare as I passed him. "If my child has nightmares about kraken chasing her, I'm going to let her call you. I don't care if it's three in the morning."

The bastard had the audacity to beam happily at me. "I just got your *child* to brush her teeth without argument for at least a month. This is the part where regular people would say, 'thank you.'"

"I guess I'm not regular."

"Maybe try some fiber."

"You're disgusting."

He cocked his head. "That's okay. You're still beautiful."

I rolled my eyes. One of the caterers used a can of lemon lime soda to refill his cup. "You don't want a shot in that?"

His smile faded. "I don't drink when there are kids around."

I glanced out onto the deck where everyone from my show was enjoying various levels of intoxication. I'd hired an entire car service to get everyone home safely.

"It's a personal preference," Jarrod said. "I don't impose it on other people."

"Why?" I asked.

"It's not my business what other people do as long as no one's getting hurt."

I gave him my "not amused" face. I knew for a fact that Jarrod drank on his film sets. Desi had told me about tequila shots in the middle of the week and a certain cooler with lots of tiny bottles inside.

Jarrod glanced around. We were alone, which I would have thought impossible with so many people invading my house.

"My father was an alcoholic," Jarrod said. There was something in his eyes. Pain? Regret? I couldn't decide what it was. "No kid needs to see that."

"Was he a mean drunk?" I asked. I couldn't handle that sad look, not in those dark eyes that always sparkled with mischief.

"Nah, he was the life of the party. He'd sing, badly. He always slaughtered the lyrics. Everyone would laugh. 'Sing us another one,' they'd say. He was too plastered to know they were laughing at him instead of with him. There's no fool like a drunken fool."

Anger crossed his face, but not disgust. The laughter hadn't bothered his father, but it had bothered Jarrod. No wonder he hated the Hollywood bad boy moniker so much. He once sued a tabloid that had published pictures of him being loaded into a taxi by his friends. He'd been too drunk to stand on his own. His suit was dismissed, but pictures like that never appeared again anywhere. I figured he had his people on it, but now I wondered if he'd stopped getting drunk in public.

"You're not drinking either." He motioned to my water.

"Someone has to be a responsible adult around here."

He shook his head. "That's not it. Are you okay?"

I ignored the question. "How do you know all the words to 'The Rainbow Connection'? Do you moonlight as a clown at kid parties?"

"My mother played the banjo. She taught me to play it. Later, when I picked up a guitar, we worked out the chords together." His attention never left my face. "You're pale, and your eyes are too bright." He tried to put his hand on my forehead. I knocked it away.

"Did I give you permission to touch me?"

"You're burning up, Sam."

"My name is Samantha."

"Yeah, I'm well aware. You've been working constantly, and your babysitter is off on vacation somewhere."

"Who told you that?" I demanded.

"You're worn out, and now you're sick."

"Go away, Jarrod. You've done enough for one night." I wasn't sure what I meant by that except that he managed to do everything better than I did, and I was sick of it.

"Go to bed."

"I have guests." But bed sounded good. I wanted to just get under my covers and forget about everything for a while. Maybe if I slept for a week, things would look better, except I couldn't do that. I had people in my house and a child to care for. I'd be up at the crack of dawn as usual.

"I'll get them where they need to go. That's kind of my thing."

"No."

"No, what?"

"No, you will not play host at my party. No, you will not play parent to my daughter. You will not waltz into my life to play house, then go back to being a man slut when you get bored." I was shouting. Why was I shouting? Everything seemed far away. Jarrod stared at me, wide eyed and concerned. He mouthed my name, but I couldn't hear him over the buzzing in my ears.

Chapter Nineteen

JARROD

"*S*ami?" She swayed. Her eyes had turned glassy. *Shit*. "Des!" I called, but she was already there. She must have come when she heard Sami shouting. Des caught Sami's arm and set the glass of ice water on the counter. Her eyes darted around like she was looking for a chair. I had a better idea. I scooped Sami up and held her against my chest. "Which way?"

I followed Desi down the hallway to the master bedroom. She tossed the decorative pillows out of the way and threw back the duvet. Sami blinked at me as I set her on the bed. "What are you doing?"

"We're taking care of you, dummy," Desi said. She produced a makeup wipe out of nowhere. "Get rid of your makeup and go to sleep. I'll have a doctor swing by first thing in the morning."

Sami started to get up. "I can't. I have stuff to do."

I removed her shoes and set them near the closet door.

Desi sat on the edge of the bed. "You need to rest before you end up in the hospital from exhaustion on top of whatever bug you managed to catch." Her tone brooked no argument. "I'll take care of things."

"You're leaving tomorrow," Sami muttered. She scrubbed clumsily with the wipe. My fingers itched to take it from her and wipe her face more gently.

"I'll leave later."

"The point is, you have people to take care of things while you get better," I said.

"I hate you," Sami said to me. Her eyes closed.

"No, you don't," Desi and I said at the same time. Desi chuckled and shook her head. She plucked the wipe out of Sami's hand and used it to clear away smeared mascara.

Sami muttered something I couldn't understand. Her eyes closed and her breathing deepened. Desi got an infrared thermometer out of the master bath and scanned Sami's forehead with it.

"Almost a hundred and two." She scowled and set the thermometer on the nightstand.

I followed Desi into the hallway.

"Where are you going tomorrow?" I asked.

"Nowhere, now," she said, frowning as she typed on her phone with her thumbs. "I can get a doctor here in the morning. She probably just needs rest."

"Where were you supposed to go?"

Desi looked up like she had only just realized I was there. "I'm supposed to meet Patrick in Dublin. His film wrapped on Thursday. There's a family reunion or something scheduled for next weekend."

"Or something?"

Desi sighed. "It's big. I'll be surrounded by Flannigans, lots and lots of them, up to my eyeballs in Irish accents. They probably all have dimples too." She gave me a smile, but I knew her too well to believe it. "I was supposed to go early to meet up with his parents and sisters before being inundated by relatives." She shook her head. Her foot tapped on the hallway tile. "It's no big deal. I'll just skip the preliminaries. That's all. We had time scheduled afterwards to spend with his parents."

"You should go."

Desi shook her head again. "Sami needs me. Carmen will be up early. Lucia isn't here to watch her."

"I can handle it. I'll get my assistant to bring anything she needs."

"If I left Sami alone with you, she'd skin me alive. Slowly. With a potato peeler." Desi's blue-gray eyes sparkled with mischief. "Then again..." She looked skyward. "I am the worst friend in the world for even considering this! Let me get a second opinion." She typed furiously on her phone. "Oliver is coming back tomorrow, so Kass will be unreachable, but I could ask her to come by in the morning."

"Des, I've got this. I can feed and entertain a not-quite-four-year-old. Sami can stay in bed. I'll find her a bell to ring if she needs anything. Hell, she might enjoy having me at her beck and call." Desi's snort of laughter was exactly what I was waiting for. "If I need backup, which I won't, I have my assistant and Sami's assistant. What's his name?"

"Evan," she said.

"Right, Evan. His number is in my phone." I pulled it out and scrolled through my contacts just to make sure.

Desi's phone chimed. She scanned the screen briefly. "Do you have Mickey's number? Their niece, Adrianna, has been watching Carmen this week."

"I met Adrianna."

"She might help too. If Sami wakes up and throws a fit about you being here, call Kassi."

I scoffed. "Kassi won't answer. Have you seen those three when they're together? A protective dome forms around them. No one else can get in."

Desi smiled, a real one this time. "Yeah, they're good that way."

That dome, the circle of safety that blocked out the rest of the world, was exactly what Kassi needed. Even I could see that.

"I don't leave until tomorrow night." Desi said. "There are a dozen things I should do in the meantime, but if you need me, just call, okay? The guest room is right here." She opened a bedroom door. "Sami always has it cleaned before these things in case someone needs to crash."

"I might not hear Carmen in the guest room. I'll take the couch." The last thing I wanted was for that sweet little girl to be scared or confused when she woke up.

Desi studied me for a moment.

"What?"

"You're a good man, Jarrod Colosi."

"Shh. Don't tell anyone. I have a reputation to protect."

Chapter Twenty

SAMI

I opened my eyes and immediately wished I hadn't. My bedroom was dark. I had light blocking shades, but my head still throbbed like a dual bass drums during a Ginger Baker solo. It took me a minute to remember the night before, that I'd bailed on my own party, and more importantly, that Lucia wasn't here to keep Carmen overnight the way she normally would. With every muscle aching like I'd been run over by a truck, I dragged myself out of bed and into the bathroom. Desi would be here. She would have stayed after clearing everyone else out. My friends wouldn't desert me. Desi was also supposed to leave for Ireland sometime soon. My head was too foggy to remember which day exactly. Either way, I'd drag myself out there and take care of my daughter so Desi could go.

Except it wasn't Desi's voice drifting down the hallway.

"You don't like bacon? I thought everybody liked bacon."

"Nope. Just pancakes with butter and syrup," Carmen said.

She had very particular opinions about, well, everything. My friends called her my mini-me. They weren't wrong. I could smell pancakes, eggs and bacon. It smelled good, but I didn't feel especially hungry.

"What about waffles?"

"They're good."

I paused in the doorway.

"Hi, mommy," Carmen said. She was dressed, and her hair had been combed into two rather lopsided and mismatched ponytails. "Jarrod's making pancakes!"

Jarrod's dark, concerned eyes landed on me. "What are you doing? You should be in bed."

"What am I doing?" I asked. "You're in my kitchen. Why are you here?" I looked around for Desi, but she was nowhere to be seen. *Traitor.*

"Are you hungry?" Jarrod asked, ignoring my question.

"Not especially." I was lightheaded, though. I leaned against the counter for support and reached for a chair. Jarrod pulled one over and guided me onto it.

"Sit down before you fall down. You're white as a sheet."

"I've never been white a day in my life," I quipped.

He rolled his eyes. "I just meant that you're pale." He hurried back to the stove and transferred some pancakes onto a plate. "Butter and syrup?" he asked Carmen.

She nodded. Jarrod smeared butter onto a pancake, poured syrup over it and cut it into squares, looking up and checking for Carmen's approval. She nodded happily. He slid the plate in front of her. "You get started on this one. I'll be back in just a minute."

"Where are you going?" she asked.

"Your mommy needs to go back to bed."

Carmen giggled. "Yeah, Mommy, go to bed."

"That's my line," I said, playing along.

Jarrod reached for my arm. I dodged. "No," I said.

"You need sleep. Desi has a doctor who makes house calls.

Your appointment is in an hour. Why don't you go back to bed until then?"

"I'm not seeing some doctor in my bedroom like an invalid," I said.

Jarrod gave me an exasperated look.

"Besides, I have work to do."

He dropped his voice down low. "You can barely stand up. Now, I have no problem carrying you to your bedroom again, but I think that might upset your daughter."

"I'll wait on the couch for the doctor. I can go back to bed later," I finally said.

Jarrod huffed a sigh, but accepted the compromise and walked with me to the living room couch. I hate to admit that I leaned on him most of the way, or that I was shivering by the time I finally sat down. Jarrod retrieved two blankets from the den and wrapped them both around me. "You are impossible," he muttered.

"Bite me," I said and clenched my teeth so they wouldn't chatter.

"When you're feeling better," he said. He laid a hand on my forehead. Whatever he felt made his frown deepened.

"Jarrod," Carmen called. "I need more syrup."

"Coming," Jarrod called back. "Can I get you anything?" he asked me.

I shook my head. My eyelids felt like lead weights. I couldn't keep them open any longer.

When I opened them again, a woman peered down at me. "There she is." Her eyebrows drew together as she studied an infrared thermometer. "Yup, definitely a fever. Are you nauseous? Upset stomach?"

I shook my head and tried to sit up.

"She was shivering earlier," Jarrod said. I glared at him just on matter of principle.

The doctor typed on her phone. "Chills, lightheaded, dizziness?"

She looked to me for confirmation. I nodded.

"The typical prescription is rest and plenty of fluids. I'll throw in an antibiotic just in case. I highly doubt it's a virus, more likely a mild infection with a bit of exhaustion thrown in for good measure." She gave me another probing look.

I tried not to appear too guilty.

"That's what I thought. Get some rest, Samantha. Try soup for lunch or dinner. In the meantime, juice, water, vitamin drinks, any liquid except dairy is good right now, but you need to rest. Okay? If you don't feel better in two days, or if you start feeling worse, call me."

I nodded, but my eyes were closing again. Jarrod could see her out. He'd let her in, apparently. I had plenty of things to say about that, but I couldn't form the words to say any of them out loud.

I woke again briefly to someone pressing a damp cloth to my forehead. Jarrod's forehead crinkled between his eyebrows. "Leave me alone," I grumbled.

"Are you awake enough to swallow a pill?" he asked. His tone was unlike anything I'd ever heard, bordering on gentle.

I propped myself up on one elbow. Jarrod positioned the pillows so I could lean against them instead of supporting myself. He handed me a glass and two pills. I swallowed one and nearly choked on the liquid. "Ugh. What is this stuff?"

"It's that stuff you give kids when they're sick."

"It's disgusting."

"Deal with it. You need the electrolytes."

"I hate you."

"Yeah, yeah. Take the damn pill and go back to sleep. I thought I was a miserable patient."

"You probably are. Most men are."

He gave me a wry smile. "Some women are too. Case in

point, you." He tapped the end of my nose. I batted his hand away.

"Where is my daughter?"

"Watching cartoons. We're going to play 'Name that Tune' Beatles edition soon."

"She likes the Beatles."

"I noticed. Is that from you or Desi?"

"All of us. Kassi bought her a Beatles lullaby CD when she was born. It was the only way I could get her to sleep most nights."

"That must have been hard, doing it all yourself." Was that admiration in his gaze? I ignored it.

"I had help. I was in a good position in my career. Most people don't have that kind of flexibility." Flexibility didn't matter when a teething baby was screaming her head off and simply would not be soothed. Those moments when I felt incompetent as a mother and just as a person in general with a good dose of exhaustion thrown in for fun, made any success I had in the creative world meaningless. I wasn't going to tell Jarrod any of that. He'd never understand that kind of hopelessness. Everything came easily to him. All he had to do was give someone that wicked smile, and they were putty in his hands.

"You're a superhero," Jarrod said, "And a goddess, which I guess makes you Wonder Woman. But even Wonder Woman needs to rest. Maybe later you can eat something?"

I regarded him suspiciously. "Maybe."

"I've been told that chicken tortilla soup is your favorite, but do you want that when you're sick?"

"Why not?"

"No idea. What a silly question. I'll order some. Go back to sleep."

I wanted to tell him to stop bossing me around, but it wasn't worth the effort. Besides, I wanted to go back to sleep.

I woke, but no baritone voice drifted through the house. I didn't hear Carmen either. It was never a good sign when I couldn't hear her. The kitchen was empty. Dishes stood in the drying rack. Everything else had been cleaned and put away. Did they go out to get lunch? I'd expected him to order in.

I could hear the television play softly in the den. Had they been watching *Hamilton*? Carmen had seen it enough times to know most of the lyrics. Jarrod sat in the corner of the couch, his head back on the cushion, sound asleep with my daughter snuggled on his lap. The way children looked when they were asleep made up for any bad behavior when they were awake. Carmen was no different. Her hand lay flat on Jarrod's chest, near her mouth. She'd never sucked her thumb, but she always slept that way with her fingers covering her lips. Jarrod had one arm around her and the other behind his head. I'd never imagined a father for Carmen. It wasn't my intention to stay single forever either, but she had always been mine. A man had never entered into the picture. But here was Jarrod of all people, sneaking past my defenses just like he always had.

I sat in a chair and just watched them for a while. This was dangerous. Jarrod and I had a contentious relationship at best. That was mostly my doing. He'd expressed his interest several times. I just kept pushing him away. What if I stopped? What if I gave him a chance? I shook my head. So many things could go wrong. Carmen could get attached to him. *I* could get attached to him. And then the next project would come along and he'd be on the other side of the world for a year, surrounded by party people, forgetting all about us. It wouldn't even take a trip around the world, just a shiny new idea, and Jarrod would be gone. I should have never let him into my life in the first place. If only he were a little less charming.

"You look awfully serious over there," Jarrod said softly.

"Are you contemplating lunch?" He lifted Carmen and shifted her off him with surprising expertise. She didn't even stir. It wasn't fair how easily all this came to him.

"Or not contemplating lunch? I didn't realize it was a controversial topic."

"What are you babbling about?"

"You, frowning at nothing." He kept his voice low and quiet. "Does my appearance upset you? I need a shave, but I didn't think I looked that bad."

"You can go home and shave," I said. "I'm okay."

"Says the woman who slept for fifteen hours straight and looks like she could sleep for fifteen more."

"Doesn't your latest gal pal miss you?" I asked. The women who had appeared at his side over the years flashed through my mind. None had lasted very long. Jarrod wasn't the type to get tied down.

"I don't have a 'gal pal' and you know it," he answered evenly.

"Surely you have more important things to do than babysit a little girl."

He stared into me with those dark eyes. "There is nothing more important than taking care of you and that sweet little girl."

My heart skipped a beat and pounded faster to make up for it. I could almost believe him. *Almost.*

Chapter Twenty-One

SAMI

arrod did take care of us. He cajoled Carmen into eating when she didn't want to, not because he had any particular skill in that area. He just managed to be more patient than I generally was. I spent most of the time in and out of sleep, but when I woke, I heard his voice and my daughter's replies. Often, they sang together, and I heard his guitar accompaniment. I overheard him talking to my assistant, Evan, on speaker, warning that I would be out of the office for at least two days. A tension deep inside me finally eased. He really did have everything under control. I could rest and get better. That was an odd feeling for me. I wanted to analyze it, but sleep kept dragging me under.

My fever finally broke Monday afternoon. I woke in semi darkness, soaked with sweat. I wanted a shower, but my legs wouldn't support me for long. I settled for fresh clothes. Jarrod heard me moving around and ended up changing the sheets on my bed while I sat in the chair and watched. I was still too shaky. His lips ghosted over my forehead as he tucked me in, and I drifted back to sleep.

The next morning, I managed to get that shower and brushed the film off my teeth. Voices met me as I came down the hall.

"Who are you and what are you doing here?" Lucia apparently had come back.

"Auntie Lucy, that's..."

"Hush. I want to know where Samantha is and why she would leave her daughter alone with you."

Jarrod answered cautiously, but I could hear the smile in his voice. "I'm Jarrod, one of Sami's friends."

Lucia harrumphed. "I've met her friends. I don't remember ever meeting you."

"Auntie." Carmen's voice grew more urgent.

"Quiet. The grownups are speaking."

"If one of the grownups would bother to listen, the *child* could explain what is going on." Children had important things to say and shouldn't be shushed. I'd gotten enough of that when I was a kid and wasn't about to do it to Carmen.

Lucia must have pushed the girls behind her when she spotted Jarrod. Emboldened by my presence, Carmen stepped between her "auntie" and her new hero. "Jarrod works with Mommy," Carmen said firmly. "He's been helping while Mommy was sick." Her resolve didn't last long under Lucia's intense stare, and my daughter ran to me.

Jarrod pulled out a chair. It was a subtle suggestion that I sit down before I fell down. I walked past him and sat, squeezing his hand as I did.

"Do you want some juice?" he asked.

I nodded. He kept a wary eye on Lucia as he poured a glass of apple juice and set it in front of me.

"You're not even dressed with a strange man in the house," Lucia scolded. "I go away, and this is what happens?"

"I've been sick," I said slowly.

"Why didn't you call me?"

Both my eyebrows shot up. *Seriously?*

"Why don't we go play outside?" Jarrod suggested to the girls.

"Okay," Carmen agreed promptly. "Come on, Maia!" They ran for the door.

Jarrod glanced back with a question in his eyes. I nodded and waved him away. I would be fine.

"Why didn't you call me?" Lucia asked again.

"When you left, I got the distinct impression you were sick of me. What was it you said?"

"I know what I said. I would have come back if you needed me."

I snorted. "You went away precisely because I needed you. There was one week of filming left and then the party. You knew exactly what you were doing."

She harrumphed again and looked out the window to where Jarrod had the girls playing some version of follow the leader. "Who is that guy?"

"He's a director."

"Oh, he's that Jarrod? I would have recognized him if he wasn't so scruffy. Doesn't he shave?"

"He's been here for two days," I said. His assistant brought clothes, but shaving must have been low on Jarrod's priority list. The top of that list, I realized, was made up of Carmen and me. That was a pleasant thought.

"He's much better looking in person," Lucia said. She glanced at me, and we both burst into laughter.

"How do I make things better?" I finally asked.

"I'm not going to Germany," Lucia said. "Maia can't change schools."

"Fine." I had expected as much and had started looking into nanny services, both in the US and Berlin.

"I want to go back to school. I need a career too."

"Fair enough," I said. "Tell me what you need, and we'll figure it out."

The answer to that took quite a while.

Chapter Twenty-Two

JARROD

"*A*rrrrgh right," I said. "The first rule of being on a pirate ship is that ye must talk like a pirate at all times, lest ye be found guilty of conduct unbecoming and forced to walk the plank."

Maia regarded me with large, dark eyes. Her face shined with excitement. Carmen giggled. I didn't think there was a huge age difference between them, two years at the most. Maia's dark hair had been woven into braids that made her look more mature. I'd managed to tame Carmen's hair into two ponytails that looked sloppy by comparison. I needed practice. Now that I was looking, Maia's outfit was perfectly coordinated and Sami probably wouldn't have left Carmen leave the house dressed as she was. I was terrible at this, but I could play act with the best of them.

"Do I hear — giggling?"

Carmen laughed harder. I heard the front door open. Sami and Lucia came out to watch.

"There's no giggling on board a pirate ship! Now who is making that giggling sound?" I leaned over to study Maia, who barely managed to suppress her grin. I stood with exaggerated precision and silly marched to Carmen who had no such control. She nearly doubled over with laughter. "Arrgh! There be a silly giggler in our midst. No pirate captain can abide a giggler. I'm afraid ye must walk the plank."

"Where's the plank?" Carmen asked.

"Right there it be. I hope ye can swim."

"I can swim," she said confidently. "Are there sharks?"

"I don't know. If there be sharks, ye'll know because first ye will hear their scary music."

Maia sang the *Jaws* theme. I saw Sami motion to Carmen, but didn't understand what passed between them.

"Are ye not afraid of walking the plank, then?" I asked.

Carmen shook her head and grinned.

"And why be that?" I asked.

She walked a narrow line, turned and did a jumping jack in the air. The sequins on her denim shorts sparkled in the sunlight. "Because I'm a mermaid!" she announced and made swimming motions to where her mother and auntie sat on the veranda.

"Oh no, a mermaid!" I said. "Be careful, first mate. Mermaids ensnare sailors with their songs. If she sings, don't listen! If you sing with her, you'll be a goner!"

Carmen still laughed uncontrollably, but managed to get out "Mahna mahna."

"Oh no," I said, over dramatizing every word. "Must. Not. Sing. Along."

"Mahna mahna," Carmen sang again.

"Curses! The long and storied career of Captain Jarrod, ended by a song sung by pink cows. I'm done for, first mate. The ship is yours." I died a long drawn out death, singing "doo doo" the whole time.

"All hail Captain Maia, the fiercest pirate in the open seas!" Sami said. She and Lucia applauded.

Carmen ran over to me. "You're not really dead," she said.

"I can be revived with a kiss." I tapped my cheek. She complied, and I jumped up, lifting her and swinging her around as I did.

"I should have recognized you," Lucia said to me. "Sami had your poster on her bedroom ceiling when we were kids."

"Luce!" Sami cried, mortified.

"Oh, really?" I drawled.

"Oh yeah, you were her favorite. In college, your picture was all over her dorm room."

"How is it I never heard about this before?" I asked.

Sami hid her face behind her hands.

"You'd think Desi would have mentioned it."

"Desi was my friend long before she was yours," Sami said. "Maybe they were her posters. Ever think of that?"

Lucia shook her head.

"Let's find out, shall we?" I pulled my phone out of my pocket.

"What time is it in Ireland?" Sami asked, as if she didn't know. She looked relieved when I put my phone away. I'd let it go for now, but no way would I forget about this. So my instincts on the plane had been correct. She was a fan, even if she hadn't been out to peddle her script.

"I'm thirsty!" Carmen said.

"Me too," Maia agreed.

Lucia led them inside, leaving us alone on the veranda.

"You still haven't eaten anything. There's waffle batter on the counter. If you're not going to use it, you should put it in the fridge."

She smiled. "You make waffles?"

"I make incredible waffles," I bragged. "But I should go. You sort everything out with your cousin?"

"I think so." She started to roll her eyes and stopped herself. "You don't have to leave."

"I do, actually. If I don't at least show my face in the office once in a while, they mobilize the search and rescue team."

"Okay then," Sami said.

"Okay then," I echoed. I wanted to chase that smile of hers forever.

It didn't take long to gather up my things and say goodbye to Lucia and the girls. I knew Desi and Kass liked me. Getting a vote of approval from Lucia was a good sign. Now, if only Sami would let me into her life on a more permanent basis, I might get to relax and be happy for a while.

She caught me outside before I reached my car. "Jarrod," she called. I turned.

"Thank you." She stepped close to me.

"It was nothing."

"It was a lot," she said and leaned in.

"Wait, are you still contagious?" I asked.

"Shut up. I hate you."

"No, you don't."

Then her arms were around my neck, and her mouth was on mine. I hadn't wanted to leave, anyway. After that, I really didn't want to go.

Chapter Twenty-Three

SAMI

I sat on the rocks and blinked in the spray as the waves broke around me. The water was cold, like always, but I'd been overheated. It felt good. It was Thursday morning, so the bike path hadn't been crowded. I hated dodging around people when I skated.

Jarrod had texted Tuesday night to make sure I was fully recovered. I didn't hear from him on Wednesday, and that bothered me more than it should. Escaping a while for intense physical activity seemed like the best way to get my head back on straight. I had promised to swing by Desi's house to check on things while she was gone. Then I'd skated from Venice to the Santa Monica pier and back again. I stowed my gear in a locker and waded out to the breakwater rocks to give my shaky muscles a chance to recover.

Sitting by the ocean was an indulgence. I went further and let my mind wander to places best avoided under normal circumstances. I remembered the way Jarrod's mouth felt on mine, the way his dark eyes went even darker, almost black, when he was aroused. I could have that again. He'd made the offer frequently enough. Even when he didn't say anything out loud, it was there in his gaze. I could have him. The problem was, I couldn't keep him. Jarrod didn't do relationships. Everyone knew that. Several women had tried to make him settle down. The details of their breakups ended up splashed on the tabloid covers for all to see. I didn't want that for myself or for Carmen. She would be starting school before long and didn't need that kind notoriety.

I climbed carefully off the rocks. The tide was coming in, and the water reached my upper thighs. It buffeted me from both sides. I looked down as I walked so I didn't trip and end up more drenched than I already was. When I finally looked up, someone was waiting on the beach. It was early, so the sun was still behind him, but I recognized the silhouette. There was a particular slouch, that perpetually bored, *I'm too cool to be standing here*, way he had of standing that I'd tried to emulate but had never quite mastered.

Once upon a time, I would have ignored him. I would have walked right past without any acknowledgment whatsoever, but that was before he nursed me through a fever and watched over my daughter for two days. Things had changed between us. Was that a good thing?

I met Jarrod's gaze squarely. Was there a flash of uncertainty behind that cocky smile? If so, it was gone in an instant. Fine. If he wanted to play, he'd caught me on the right day for it.

"What are you doing here?" I asked, only feigning mild interest instead of my usual exasperation.

"I wanted to show off my moves at the skate park, but there wasn't much of an audience."

I raised one eyebrow.

"I was looking for you, of course," he said. He offered a bottle of water.

I took it. Despite the time he'd spent at my house, there was no domestic bliss in our future. We'd never eat breakfast together before going about our days like Desi and Patrick did. There would be no house shopping or remodeling like Kassi enjoyed with her men. Jarrod and I would be destined for a weekend here, an evening there. I didn't want that.

But he was giving me that cocky grin, the one that could make my panties disappear in a puff of steam. One more time. I could give in one last time to get over him and get back to work. I'd tried this before, with little success, but things were different now. Weren't they? "I have to get my bag from the locker."

"Okay."

He followed me without a word. I had two bags jammed into the locker, a backpack with my inline skates, and another with a change of clothes and shower supplies. There were public showers and changing rooms here at the beach, but I had a better alternative. Jarrod offered to carry my duffle, and I let him. We paused at a bench close to the boardwalk, and I used baby powder to un-stick the sand from my legs.

"Huh. I never would have thought of that," he said.

"It's this or have sand all over my car from every trip to the beach," I said. I didn't mention Carmen out of habit.

"You must be hungry. We could get lunch?" He glanced at his ridiculously expensive watch. "Or brunch?"

"I'm disgusting," I said simply.

"I could follow you to your place," he suggested. "Or we could go to mine?"

I gave him side eye. His house was in the hills and, no. Just no. "There's another alternative," I said, and let him follow me down the boardwalk. I'd bought the condo as an investment. It had been a good one. The income I got from renters well exceeded any expenses, and there were times when it was empty, and I could use it.

"Doesn't Desi live around here?" he asked, as if he didn't

know exactly which corner in Santa Monica Desi called home.

"A bit north, but that's not where we're going."

"Oh." He hefted the bag. "Do you always pack an overnight bag when you go skating?"

"Do you always ask so many questions?"

His mouth closed with a click. That was the thing. Jarrod didn't ask random questions. He preferred to observe silently and inquire only pointedly to get to what he wanted. The difference was he wasn't in control of this situation. I was. I studied him covertly. He seemed on edge. Good.

I pulled my keys from the pocket of my pack as we climbed the stairs. His dark eyes darted around as we entered the condo. He was immediately drawn to the picture window looking out on the ocean. "Nice view," he said.

Everyone said that.

"Is this place yours?"

"It is."

He took in the bright, seaside colors and happy decorations. They weren't my style, but the renters loved them. The whole place was bright and airy. I liked that.

"I'm taking a shower. Relax, watch TV, whatever," I said.

"Or I could join you."

I turned back. Jarrod watched me. He knew I'd refuse. That was written on his face. He kept his expression mostly neutral, *just making a suggestion,* it said. He seemed to try for innocuous, but his dark eyes danced with mischief. He thought he was keeping me off balance. He didn't know whom he was playing with.

"Wait until five minutes after you hear the water. Then you can come in."

His eyes went wide. I turned quickly to hide my smile and shut the master bath door behind me.

Chapter Twenty-Four

JARROD

I waited to hear the click of the lock, but it never came. There had to be a catch. Sami wouldn't agree that easily. I examined the past few minutes, then went all the way back to the beach. She'd looked so beautiful with the ocean spray splashing up around her. I heard water, but no, that wasn't a shower. Probably the sink instead. Was it creepy to stand here listening? It was. I went to the window. The master bedroom faced the water, too. What did Sami do with this place? Was it a child free location for trysts? No, that wasn't her style. More likely, it was an investment. We weren't supposed to talk about money, but I knew what each of the three *Death Sucks* writers were worth and how they'd built their fortunes. Desi was cautious because her divorce had dumped her back at square one. Kassi had been on her own since she was sixteen, and worked her ass off to ensure she had enough to keep her secure for the rest of her life. But Sami, she'd created an empire. She had her fingers in any number of pies, and from what I could tell, most of them paid large dividends. Carmen would be able to go to whatever college she chose and travel the world before and after if she wanted. There were few secrets in Hollywood, even if Sami guarded her private life better than anyone I'd ever met.

I heard the shower and glanced at my watch. Five minutes. Should I just walk in there naked? What was Sami expecting? She probably wanted the time to wash up before I invaded her space. I didn't want to wait. The image of running a soapy cloth over her light brown skin danced through my head. Maybe not this time, but someday... What was I thinking? Sami wouldn't agree to more than an afternoon fling. And maybe she was right. I wasn't ready for a family, no matter how appealing the idea of the three of us was.

I checked my watch. No point in worrying about what could or couldn't be in the future when I could have her right now. I kicked off my shoes and pulled off my socks. There was no sexy way to remove one's socks. I'd figured that out as a teenager. Something, call it insecurity or ego, wouldn't let me just walk into the bathroom naked, like I was entitled to whatever came next. I opened the door slowly and peered around it. The shower door was frosted, and all I could see was the silhouette of Sami's slim frame.

"Will you get in here?" Her voice had an impatient snap in it. It turned gentle when she said, "We shouldn't waste water."

I pulled my shirt over my head and pushed my jeans and boxer briefs to the floor in one motion. She couldn't see me any better than I could see her, but I felt her gaze. When I opened the shower door, she was turned away, and I got a view of her dark hair heavy with water, hanging down her back almost to her prefect, round ass. I had spanked that ass until it grew hot under my hand, then gripped it as she rode me and then again when I took her from behind. The memories, never buried as deep as I'd like, resurfaced hard enough to freeze me where I stood. It took Sami turning to stare at me, her amber eyes demanding, to get me moving again.

"You're letting the warm air out," she said.

I stepped into the shower and closed the door behind me. I had to look at her, from her pert breasts and brown nipples, down her flat stomach and narrow hips.

Chapter Twenty-Five

SAMI

*J*arrod stared at me like he wanted to kneel at my feet. I'd never seen him that way, almost worshipful. It wasn't entirely comfortable. He was gloriously naked. It had been a while since I'd last seen him like this. On screen didn't count, and I certainly didn't watch his nude scenes late at night on my laptop.

I let my gaze run over him. My fingers twitched to touch his chest. I wanted to tease his nipples with my tongue just to see his reaction. Maybe I wouldn't start with his chest. His legs were pretty solid, too. I could run my fingers up the outside of his thighs until I reached what I really wanted. It jutted out, hard and ready.

"Like what you see?" Jarrod asked.

I raised my eyes to meet his. "Maybe." For an instant, I wished he was wearing a shirt so I could ball it in my fist and pull him to me. Why was he hanging back? I closed the space between us and slid my arms around his neck. There was something to be said for skin to skin contact. My arousal skyrocketed the moment I leaned into him. His skin was still cool. I was warm from the shower and even more heated by

Jarrod's proximity. My lips found his. That kiss held all kinds of pent up frustration, as if it had been building in both of us for the last two years. In truth, it had been. I wanted to wrap myself around him. Forget waiting. Forget going slow. I wanted him now. I flexed my hips so his cock was tight between us. Jarrod groaned.

"I want you," I breathed. I was about to wrap my leg around his hip, but he spun me around and held me tight with his arm under my breasts. I could feel his erection hard and hot in my lower back. His right hand slid down my hip and between my legs, finding my clit so easily, it was like he'd practiced the move. I didn't want to think about that, and then I could barely think at all because he was really good at this. He trailed kisses from my shoulder up my neck and tongued the sensitive area behind my earlobe. All the while, his fingers circled my clit and teased my entrance until I was squirming, trying to draw him in.

"You know I want you, Sami. I always want you." He slid two fingers inside me and curled them forward, hitting that magical spot while his thumb strummed my clit. I'd seen Jarrod play a guitar. I knew his hands were talented, but, *damn*. He knew what he was doing. It was too easy for him to stoke the fire under my skin. He held me tight while his wicked fingers pushed me closer to the edge, and yeah, the strength in his grip turned me on that much more. I dug my fingers into his arm. My other hand gripped his hair. I turned my head, and his lips found mine. He wouldn't let me turn around. His right hand moved faster, and I couldn't think anymore. That delicious tension coiled tighter and tighter until it finally broke. My hips bucked. I moaned. Jarrod held me as I came back to earth.

"I can't wait to taste you again," he said.

I leaned back into him, unsure that my legs could support me. He reached around and turned off the water. I probably could have stood on my own, but it was nice being that close, nicer still when he wrapped me in a fluffy towel and used another to squeeze the water out of my hair. I wasn't accustomed to this kind of care. Last time, we'd fallen away from each other, panting and covered in sweat. It had been that intense. This time, I felt Jarrod's attention like an additional layer on my skin. He'd been like this when I was sick, watching me closely the whole time. Was this the real Jarrod under all the cocky layers?

"Come on," he said. "Don't make me wait any longer." He caught my hand and led the way to the bed. Despite his urgency, he stretched out and kissed me like he'd be content to just do that for hours. When I arched into him, he slowed us both down. His tongue found sensitive spots on my neck and lower. He cupped my breasts and teased until I writhed under him. I plunged my hands into his hair and pulled him tighter. I couldn't get close enough.

He drew back. "Put your arms up above your head. Hold onto the edge of the mattress."

I let a sultry smile cross my face. "Why, Mr. Colosi, do you want to tie me up?"

His lips found mine again. I must have moved too slowly for his taste, because he guided my arms where he wanted them. "If we were at my house, I'll pull out the leather cuffs."

"Kinky," I said.

"You love it."

"I do," I admitted. Nothing wrong with that.

"Behave yourself, and I'll make you come."

"As if you ever wouldn't. Admit it, you get off on getting me off." I arched my back. This was a great look, with my arms above my head.

"Fuck," he whispered. "You're beautiful."

I smiled.

"You don't know what you do to me," he said.

"I have an idea." I caught his hand and put it between my legs so he could see how he affected me, then slipped my hand back under the pillow. I was wet in a way that had nothing to do with just having showered.

Jarrod groaned, but he kept teasing me. His fingers barely delved into my swollen folds. I wanted to force my will over his, but I played the game and pretended to be bound. His mouth finally closed over my clit and I nearly floated off the bed. How could I walk away from this? I could always find a willing partner, but this electricity, like a building thunderstorm, only happened with Jarrod.

He drew it out. His fingers, lips and tongue moved in perfect coordination, all designed to bring me close to that edge, but not push me over. What was he waiting for? Did he want me to beg? I moaned his name and tried to get closer. He sucked my clit hard, drawing it over his teeth, and the world went blank.

"You're right, you know," he said. His deft fingers massaged my arms, even my hands and fingers as if I really had been bound.

"I'm always right," I said. "But about what specifically?"

"I do get off on getting you off."

He must have set a condom on the nightstand before getting in the shower. It hadn't been there before. Once he put it on, all bets were off. Jarrod loved to try different positions. I remembered that from last time, but he used a few more this time around. I wondered if he'd been studying the *Kamasutra*.

He didn't give up control like before. I had to fight him for it. He pinned my hands to the mattress. I laced my fingers through his, dug my heels into the small of his back, and lifted my hips, forcing my rhythm over his. He growled, but I could tell he enjoyed it. Likewise, when I was on top, he guided my hips, forcing me to slow down, and laughed at my frustration.

"I'll get you for this," I panted.

He flipped us so he was back on top. "I do hope so."

Sex was never a sweet surrender with Jarrod. The fire burned too hot between us for that. It scorched my nerves and muscles, leaving me limp and shaking. Would a relationship with him be the same way, with both of us struggling for the upper hand? We'd end up miserable, though several mind blowing orgasms made me wonder if it would be worth a try.

"Look at me, Sami."

No, that was dangerous. Did he realize the way he looked at me? Adoration and desire battled in his gaze. I told myself it was an act. He'd probably looked at a dozen women that way and sent them home the next morning. The papers called him a consummate bachelor. I had to remember that or risk getting my heart broken.

He pushed my hair off my forehead. "Sam." His dark eyes searched mine. I didn't want him to see what I was thinking. There was no scenario in which he would be mine. I used my leg muscles to flip us over. He wasn't expecting it. If he had been, I probably wouldn't have been able to do it. I was strong, but Jarrod outweighed me by fifty pounds at least. I didn't give him a moment to protest, just gyrated my hips fast and hard. He moaned an objection, but I wasn't having any of it. I leaned back so his cock stroked my g-spot and reached back between his legs. His balls had drawn up tight, making it that much easier for me to find the sensitive spot behind them. I stroked that nerve center and he cried out. His back bowed. So did mine as one last orgasm rushed through me. Part of it could have been the power trip. I got off on getting him off, too.

I fell onto the bed next to him. "I'm going to need another shower," I said.

"You're on your own this time. I need a nap. And food. Have lunch with me?"

"You want more?" I asked. "That wasn't enough to get me out of your system?" As soon as I said it, I wished I hadn't.

Jarrod's smile disappeared. I'd managed to rip away his sleepy contentment. Shock flashed in his eyes, followed by pain. It was gone a moment later, replaced by the cocky half smirk he always had ready for the cameras. "You're projecting a little, don't you think?"

He bounded off the bed in a sudden burst of energy and disappeared into the bathroom. He emerged moments later, fully dressed, not a hair out of place.

"That was fun," he said, picking up his shoes and socks, but not stopping to put them on. "I'll see you around, okay?"

"Jarrod," I said. I didn't want to sit there naked, but we hadn't bothered to remove the bedspread. There was no convenient way to wrap myself in a sheet and chase after him.

He left without saying goodbye.

Chapter Twenty-Six

JARROD

I put my phone in airplane mode and left it there. There was work to do, a script to read through and mark up, plans to make, schedules to coordinate. I had a team that worked on my projects, along with a list of crew that I trusted. It was just a matter of bringing everyone on board and getting pre-production started. Isaac, my office manager, didn't even bother to hide his surprise when I walked through the doors early on Friday after being there late the night before. I never came in on Fridays. He saw my personal assistant more often than he saw me. I'd thought for a while there had been a romance brewing there, but now I wasn't so sure. Gavin's schedule was impossible, mostly because my schedule was impossible, and he followed me most places. Isaac had a military background, so a changeable schedule should be nothing new. But what did I know? I'd thought Sami wanted me in her life, or at least that she had considered it.

"That wasn't enough to get me out of your system?" Seriously? Okay, I'd signed on to direct an episode of *Death Sucks* with the intention of getting over Sami, but... There was no but.

She'd just said what I'd been thinking, except I'd stopped thinking it after a single day on set. Maybe even earlier. Get her out of my system. How could I do that? She'd been a permanent resident in my thoughts since that damn flight from New York to Los Angeles.

I'd tried to explain away my obsession. I felt guilty for acting like an arrogant ass. She hurt my ego by rejecting my attempt to apologize and then again by backing out of the project. There was an element of truth to both of those excuses. I'd done a lot during that production to get Sami back on board, flowers, fruit baskets, custom M&M's with "sorry" printed on each piece of candy. I'd looked into her career and, like a fanboy stalker, read every interview and watched the recording of her commencement speech when she was given an honorary doctorate. The internet had plenty indicators of her likes and dislikes. When I saw something I imagined would make her smile, I bought it and sent it via courier to her office. There had been a new writer on the production, but I'd wanted Sami to consult. She'd never responded, not once. I hadn't known she was pregnant and on bed rest. If I had... Maybe I would have run away screaming instead of snatching up a screenplay written by one of her best friends.

Sami had contacted me then. I never asked how she got my number, but her texts came fast and furious from preproduction through the wrap party. After the wrap party, after that night, which I was trying desperately not to remember, there had been radio silence again until I bought the film rights to Kassi's novel and found the funding to get it made. It was a good story, good enough to earn an armload of Oscars, but I'd been looking for Sami's attention, not awards. And now, were we back to where we'd been after that first night? I had optioned a sequel to Kassi's film based on her second novel in the series, but I wasn't ready to go down that road again, not yet anyway.

"That wasn't enough to get me out of your system?" I threw the pen I'd been using across the room. It hit the chair instead of the wall. Nothing satisfying about that. I wanted to break something. Maybe I should go for a run and burn off excess energy. If only thoughts of Sami, her scent, her taste, the way her skin warmed under my touch, wouldn't follow me the entire way. Beyond the physical, I loved sparring with her. I loved her statement t-shirts and the wicked glint in her whiskey colored eyes when she needled me. She was so damn smart. The work I'd done on *Death Sucks* was some of the best I'd done in years, all because I was trying to compete with her. And what about Carmen? God, that kid had me wrapped around her adorable little finger. It was as effortless for her as for her mother. And now I was supposed to just forget about them when, for a day or two, I'd been picturing the three of us together as a family? This was pathetic. I was pathetic. I raked my fingers through my hair, pulling it as I did. As always, the pain helped me focus. I opened the script and started reading.

"Uh, Jarrod?"

I looked at the clock first. Barely an hour had passed. This day was never ending. Isaac stood in the doorway. He was in pain and doing his best not to show it. I recognized the tightness around his mouth. He leaned on his cane. He'd gotten pretty good at only using it for balance, but this was different.

"What's up?" I asked.

"I might have screwed up."

"Am I broke now?"

He relaxed and even smiled a little.

"Are we talking sell the car collection broke, or get a cardboard box and take up residence next to my star on Hollywood Boulevard broke?"

Isaac did laugh at that. "Nothing like that." He shifted to lean against the door jamb. He really was uncomfortable. Isaac didn't slouch. "I just confirmed to Samantha Augustine that you were here. It was unintentional."

"She can be very persistent," I said. I had experienced that myself. "What happened?"

"I think she's coming here. She said Gavin told her where you were."

Sami's assistant Evan had told me where to find her on Venice Beach, so I had no right to be angry with Gavin. Turnabout was fair play. "Did the conversation end with her saying 'ah, so he is there' right before she hung up?"

"Something very close to that, yes," Isaac said.

"Not your fault, then. We should send her to Quantico to train interrogators. She could teach the experts a thing or two."

"I think she's coming here."

The front door chime sounded, and we both looked.

"What do you want me to do?" Isaac asked in an urgent whisper.

Chapter Twenty-Seven

SAMI

arrod's production office was nice. The colors were a step up from industry neutral. Someone had managed to make the framed movie posters look tasteful and even a little elegant. We had similar artwork in our writers' room, but it looked more like a college dorm room than an office. The candy and toys might have had something to do with that, too. Jarrod's main area sported a nice desk and only a few chairs. I could see a conference room on one side. That would be the proverbial room where it happened, though the real work would be done on a computer somewhere. I wondered where that room was.

A man in his late twenties stood in a doorway. The door was mostly closed. He blocked the opening. I thought he might have a prosthetic leg. He had military posture, but either the prosthetic was new, or he was having a bad day. It wasn't obvious, but my job was to notice stuff like that.

"You must be Isaac."

"That's right," he said. He wanted to "yes, ma'am" me. I could tell. That sort of talk didn't do well in Hollywood. I wasn't old enough to be called "ma'am" by anyone.

"And I bet that's Jarrod's office."

"I can't let you in," he said. He was definitely former military. That stoic mask was the sort of thing they learned in basic.

"But I brought lunch. There's enough for five people at least," I said and gave him wide eyes. "Don't you want lunch?"

"Tell her, 'no girls allowed,'" Jarrod said from within.

I fought a smile and lost. He was here. There had been the chance that I'd show up like a sad, desperate supplicant while Jarrod ducked out the back. I set the restaurant bags on the desk and leaned against the edge.

"Now where's the fun in that?" I asked. I could just picture Jarrod's face as he scrambled for a reply.

"Tell her, 'bros before...'"

"I can't say that!" Isaac interrupted, looking back over his shoulder, aghast.

I liked this guy.

"Okay," I sighed and reached for the bags. "Tell Jarrod I brought a peace offering, but if he doesn't want dessert from *La Chouquette*, I'll just take it home with me."

"You could leave the food, you know." Jarrod appeared behind Isaac. "A proper peace offering would just be left at the gates."

"A proper peace offering involves a giant horse with a lot of Greek soldiers inside it," I said.

Isaac probably found this exchange infinitely amusing, but he controlled his features. Only his brown eyes sparkled.

"That wasn't a peace offering. It was a trick to get inside the walls. I see what's really going on here." Jarrod narrowed his eyes at me.

"I'm hungry, even if you aren't," Isaac said, looking with interest at the bags I carried. He strode to his desk with precise steps. I pretended not to notice the cane.

"Traitor," Jarrod muttered.

"Come on, Isaac. I didn't know what you liked, so I got a little of everything. Since Jarrod wants to hide in his office, you get first choice." I set anything that piqued his interest on his desk and added a chocolate éclair for dessert. "Take whatever's left home for dinner. Actually," I glanced at Jarrod. "I think you deserve the afternoon off."

"Yeah, okay," Isaac said with a laugh.

"See? I'm much nicer than he is. You should work for me," I stage whispered.

"Hey! No stealing my people," Jarrod called.

"Did he tell you that he made movies with both of my writers?" I asked. "And he accuses me of stealing people?" I really needed a folding fan for this act.

"Go home, Isaac," Jarrod said.

Isaac looked back at Jarrod, surprised. "Are you sure?"

"She's right, you do deserve it."

I grinned, packed the food into a bag, and sent Isaac on his way with enough to feed him for the entire weekend.

"So, a peace offering, eh?" Jarrod said as he selected a container and started eating. Gavin had advised me on the restaurant and Jarrod's favorite menu items. Gavin had also suggested bribing Isaac to get in the door. Pretty ingenious, which was probably why Jarrod hired him.

As for Jarrod, he sat at his desk. I sat across from him in a chair reserved for guests. The distance between us wasn't just physical. He glanced at me between bites and ate like he was starving. I poked my own food with a fork, but couldn't bring myself to eat.

"Look, I'm sorry. I..." My teeth snapped together. I'd rehearsed and discarded a dozen lines on the way over. None of them seemed convenient now.

Jarrod's eyebrows rose. "You were saying?"

"Has anyone ever called you domineering?"

"Duh, I'm a director." He poked at his food. "I like to be in control."

"Maybe I want to be in control."

"Okay." He said that casually, as if we were commenting on the weather.

"I mean, your way is fun, but... wait, what?"

He took a drink before he answered. "I said, okay. You want control, you can have it." He looked up and caught me in his gaze. "Name the time and the place. I'll kneel at your feet if that's what you want."

"No, you wouldn't." I scoffed.

He leaned forward. His dark eyes burned. "Try me."

I forgot to breathe for a long moment. I spotted a script on his desk. "What's that?"

"My next project." He didn't sound enthused.

"May I?" I reached for the script. He motioned with his fork. I scanned the pages. "So, car chase, lots of explosions, one page of dialogue, shoot out, another car chase, more explosions. Your budget must be huge."

"It's a logistical nightmare."

"You don't like it?"

"It will make me a lot of money."

"You already have a lot of money." Who was he kidding? He didn't have to work for the money anymore. He glared at the script in my hand like he loathed the thing. "When do you start?" I asked.

"I'm supposed to go to Thailand in a month to scout locations."

"Aren't there actual location scouts for that? You know people who take pictures and send them to you?"

"I like to see it for myself."

I said, "Control freak," and covered it with a fake sneeze, but I understood why he would want to see everything for himself. I probably would too. "Why not do something else? You have an Oscar. Offers must be pouring in."

"So I'm a control freak and a man slut. Anything else?" He drank some water. The corners of his mouth twitched. "Come to think of it, isn't that a tad sexist? By calling me a man slut, you implied that sluts are by default women. That's messed up."

I stared at him. He'd turned on the charm. Maybe I hadn't scared him away. "I never called you a man slut. You must have me confused with one of your other girlfriends."

His smile widened. Crap, did I just call myself his girlfriend?

"I think the exact statement was something about waltzing into your life and then going back to being a man slut, which, again, implies..."

"All right, I get it!" I said. "In a moment of aggravation, I used a stupid term to describe your libertine lifestyle."

"Oh, libertine, that's even better." He laughed. "You would be surprised how few women I've been with in the past four years."

"It's none of my business," I said and fiddled with the paper fasteners on the script.

"Ask me why."

I glanced at him and quickly away before he could trap me in that intense gaze. "Are you getting a lot of offers?" I asked instead.

Since I'd dodged his question, he did the same with mine. "What about you? Rumor is that you're doing a limited series with a certain premium cable network."

"Well, if there are rumors, then it has to be true." I said. He was leaving in a month. I'd be in Germany for nearly five months. There was no way for this to work. Why was I even here? I set the script down and retreated to his couch. There was another script on a side table there.

"Rumor has it that the limited series with the certain premium network will be filming in Berlin," he said.

"What of it?" I thumbed through that script, scanning the pages.

"Is your cousin going too?"

"Probably not." I sighed.

"I guess that's to be expected."

"Why?" I asked. My anxiety rose every time I thought about Germany. I'd need to hire a nanny to come with us. It would be complicated, and what if she didn't work out and Carmen had to adjust to yet another person in addition to living in a strange country where everyone spoke a different language?

"Maia's older. She must be in school, right?" He left his food behind and joined me on the couch. "Hey, what's wrong?"

"Nothing. I'll figure it out."

"Of course you will. Carmen will have you listening to German opera. She'll probably be able to translate it too. Kids pick up languages quickly."

He could only be so calm because he wasn't a parent. I told myself that, even as the surety in his voice soothed my nerves. He really believed that everything would work out. I could almost believe it, too.

He tucked my hair behind my ear. "Let me spend the weekend with you."

"You stayed at my house last weekend." I read the script in my hands to avoid looking at him.

"That doesn't count. Let's spend some actual time together. We'll drive up the coast. Carmen would love riding in a convertible."

"She probably would," I said absently. I scanned another page. "What is this?"

"I bought the rights to that a long time ago. Couldn't get the funding to make it."

I read some more. "But this is good."

"I know," he agreed. "No money, no movie."

"Jarrod, you have an Oscar. If you want funding, just ask for it." Awards opened all kinds of doors and he had a shelf full of them for directing Kassi's film.

He looked at me like the idea had never occurred to him, as if he had given up on this project, the one he wanted, and accepted that he had to do what the studios dictated instead.

"There's nothing wrong with big budget action films." I had several in my movie library. "But this one is important. Wouldn't it be better to make a film that mattered?"

"I already have crews under contract for that one," he said, nodding toward his desk. "You know what it's like to have people depend on you. I can't just hop from one project to another and leave my teams hanging."

"And you don't know any other directors who would jump at a project like that, especially with qualified crews already in place?" I studied him. "It's not like you to take the easy route."

He leaned back, away from me. "How would you know what is 'like me' and what isn't?"

I blinked. There was something there, some pain from people and the press making assumptions about him. I realized the very last thing I wanted was for Jarrod to look at me that way, as if I was like everyone else. I'd seen the real Jarrod Colosi, the one who strummed the guitar and hummed to himself long after his audience of one had fallen asleep on the couch. I'd heard him laugh at my daughter's jokes as he made pancakes. Even if a relationship between us couldn't work, I wanted to stay in his inner circle because I suspected he let very few people get that close.

"I've followed your career, Jarrod," I said. "Closely. I had a poster of you on the ceiling above my bed, after all."

He looked skyward and laughed. "What I would have paid for that information a few years ago."

"Well, you have it now," I said. "Congratulations."

I watched his tension drain away. That mischievous grin was back. I would have preferred he not know about that poster, but it was worth sacrificing my dignity to see him smile again.

"Spend the weekend with us," I said, smoothing his hair. It stuck up in places like he'd been raking his fingers through it. I'd seen him do that on set when he was frustrated. Desi said that was the reason he wore that fedora, to keep him from pulling his hair. The item in question hung among others on an actual hat rack in the corner. He saw me looking.

"Stay away from my hat."

I chuckled and finished fixing his hair instead. He leaned into my touch, and his eyelids lowered to half-mast. If he'd been a cat, he would have purred. *Interesting.* "Spend with weekend with us," I said again and leaned in to speak directly into his ear. "It's been a while since I rode in a convertible too."

He shivered and pulled back enough to look at me. We were so close, our noses almost touched.

"Ask me why," he said.

"You've been working non-stop for the past four years," I said. "You didn't have time for a relationship." I tried to remember if I had seen his name linked to any Hollywood starlets over the past four years. There had been rumors, but they had been debunked by the same tabloids that had printed them in the first place.

"That didn't sound like a question to me."

I huffed out a breath. Why were we still talking? I wanted

him right here in his office on his couch. It was naughty and dangerous, and that just increased the appeal. "Why haven't you been with many—"

"Any," he corrected.

I sputtered a laugh. "You mean to tell me you've been living like a monk for four years? I don't believe you."

He shrugged. "You're right, I have been working constantly, and it's not like I haven't gotten offers."

"Of course you have," I said. "You're Hollywood's most eligible bachelor."

He rolled his eyes at that. "There are places to go and play, but actual sex was never part of that for me. And I haven't even been to any of them in a while. My memberships might have lapsed."

"Why are you telling me this?"

"Ask the question."

His dark eyes bored into mine. I was suddenly afraid of the answer. "Why haven't you been with anyone in the past four years?" But he had been with someone. He'd been with me the night of Desi's wrap party.

"Because ever since that flight from New York to L.A., that first time you walked away from me, I haven't been able to get you out of my head." He twirled one of my curls around his finger and stared at that rather than my face. "I've been chasing you ever since, and you keep walking away. That night of the party, any time I tried to talk to you on set, then again yesterday..."

"You were the one who left yesterday," I said.

He met my gaze then. "You pushed me away yesterday, and you know it."

Of course I had. I put distance between us before he had the chance. I'd never dreamed he'd actually been waiting for me. I thought I was just a challenge, that rare woman who said "no" to Jarrod Colosi.

"I told you, I'll go away, if that's what you want."

"I don't want you to go away," I said. The words came out in a rush, as if some dam had broken and I couldn't hold them back anymore.

"So you don't hate me?" he teased. "Because I distinctly remember being told numerous times..."

I plunged my fingers into his thick, dark hair and pulled him to me. He tried to drag me onto his lap. I straddled him instead.

"Truce?" I asked.

Jarrod stood, taking me with him so I stood too. He spun me around, unfastened my jeans, pulled them over my hips, and pulled me back down onto his lap before I could react. His hands slid up under my shirt to cup my breasts. I leaned back against him and sighed.

"Peace talks come after the battles are finished," he said, his lips against my neck. One of his hands dropped between my legs to tease me there. I lifted my hips. I wanted more. Jarrod nipped the place where my neck and shoulder joined, but back where any mark would be hidden. My back bowed. "Let's face it, you and I enjoy the fight entirely too much to call a truce so soon."

His voice made me vibrate like a tuning fork. No one had ever done that before. How he managed to open his jeans and put on a condom was a mystery, but it was there when he lifted me and positioned his cock between us. I reached down and guided him where I wanted him to go. The fingernails of my right hand dug into his thigh as he entered me, but he didn't seem to mind. My jeans were around my thighs, preventing me from getting much leverage, but that's the way Jarrod liked it. He liked taking control. Sometimes, I liked letting him have it.

"Aren't you glad I sent Isaac home?" I gasped, unable to

stop taunting him, even when I was in a compromising position.

His sigh sounded more like a growl. He rocked his hips, thrusting into me. "What am I going to do with you?"

"Oh, I'm sure you'll think of something." We didn't say anything else for a while.

PART THREE

"Shameless"

Chapter Twenty-Eight

JARROD

I spent the next two weeks vacillating between a deep, unfamiliar sense of peace and an edgy feeling that I couldn't quite shake.

Sami and I both had plenty of work to occupy our days. I had always loved my job. Even the worst day on a set was better than the best day at a corporation. I still believed that, but as much as I tried to focus on my next project, I just couldn't summon any interest. Usually, I could see the story clearly and it was just a matter of making my vision reality. This time, it was just words on a page. I tried starting in the middle or going backwards from the final scene. Nothing could bring it to life. I went through the motions, making lists and breaking down scenes, but it felt soulless and robotic. Every day in my office felt like a prison sentence. I counted the hours until I could escape and meet up with Sami and Carmen.

We went for late afternoon walks on the beach and ate dinner in casual restaurants I would have never considered visiting before. Sami and I walked, both of us holding

Carmen's hands. "One, two, three!" she counted. On three, we swung her high between us, and she laughed. I had grown to love that sound. I found bliss with them that I would have sworn didn't exist off screen.

We spent the evenings eating popcorn and watching Pixar movies. I had some time alone with Sami after Carmen went to bed before I left and returned to my cold, empty house. I tried to remember what I was thinking when I bought it, probably something about the view and how impressive it looked on the drive in. There were rooms I'd never even used. What a waste. Sure, I'd hosted gatherings, lots of them. I could send out a call and strangers would appear, excited and ready to party, but how was that better than Sami's quiet humming and Carmen's endless chatter? I was tired of being surrounded by strangers. My house was cold and sterile. It felt like it belonged to someone else.

Weekends were different. I stayed with them Friday night, and we planned an outing for Saturday. Sami accused me of spoiling her daughter, because I gave in way before any tantrum started. All Carmen had to do was turn her big brown eyes on me, and I crumbled every single time.

We walked out of a restaurant after lunch, and the real world poked at our happy bubble. "Paparazzi at two o'clock," I warned Sami.

"What's poparocksee?" Carmen asked.

"It's another word for reporter," Sami explained. "See the man over there with the camera? He won't bother us. He just wants to take pictures."

"He's a reporter?"

"Yes."

Carmen broke away from us and ran down the sidewalk. Sami shouted her name.

"Hey!" Carmen said, running right up to the reporter. "She's my mommy, and you don't get that part of her."

He snapped a picture of Carmen's outraged little face. I could feel Sami growl, but my legs were longer. I got there first.

"Samantha Augustine is your mother?" he asked Carmen.

I lifted her from behind and spun to pass her off to Sami. The reporter watched this with interest.

"Hey, I'll give you," I looked down to see what I had in my pocket, "three hundred dollars if you delete those pictures and forget about this."

"You're kidding, right? A secret kid is huge. I'll get paid way more than three hundred for this story."

"Whatever they're paying you, I'll double it." I pulled out my phone. "I'll transfer the money right now."

"Is she yours?"

I wish she was. I shut my mouth tight before the words could escape. "What will it take to keep this off the internet?"

"Jarrod, it's okay," Sami said. I noticed she kept Carmen's face shielded from the camera. "It was going to come out eventually."

I sighed and regarded the reporter. "Will you show me the pics?"

He didn't release his camera, but scrolled through the pictures. There were a few where Carmen was turned away from the camera. The last one, of Carmen storming up to the camera made me smile. I added my business card to the cash. "Do me a favor. Send the ones that don't show her face to your editor. Pretend the others don't exist. Except that last one. Send that to me." I held out the money. "Deal?"

He went through and deleted all but the pictures I specified. I watched him do it. There might be a way to recover them, but I didn't think so. I handed over the money. My card listed my email. Carmen looked just like her mother in that last photo. I had to have it. "If you want a job doing something else, contact me," I said.

He nodded. I put my arm around Sami and leaned in to kiss her forehead as we walked away. "It will be all right."

"Of course it will." She didn't sound too sure.

I checked the internet later that night, and stories of Sami's secret child were everywhere. Someone found the hospital records, and every article pointed out that no father's name was given. The only positive thing was that the pictures didn't show Carmen's face. The photographer had kept his promise.

Sami had been looking over my shoulder as I read on my tablet at the kitchen table. She sank into the chair next to me. "I knew it wouldn't last forever. They'll follow us everywhere now. I probably made it worse by keeping her hidden all this time."

"It'll blow over," I assured her. "Some couple will split or get married and take the attention away from you. I could call in a favor, have some friends get into a fight in a restaurant, if you like."

She smiled just a little. "I should have broken his camera," Sami said. "I wanted to knock him flat."

"The story would have still gotten out, and you'd have a lawsuit to deal with on top of it." That didn't seem to help, so I added, "And Carmen would have gotten upset. No point in making her afraid of the press. You handled it perfectly by ignoring him."

"You don't think punching a reporter would be setting a good example?"

"Let's wait until she's a little older before we teach her to punch people, don't you think?"

Sami stared at me like I'd grown a second head, and only then did I realize what I'd said. That pronoun, "we" carried with it a world of promise and the opportunity for complete, abject failure.

I steered the conversation to safer topics. Carmen's birthday was around the corner. Sami was against ridiculous parties that were more about the adults in attendance than the child. She'd do something special with Lucia and Maia on the actual day, and get together with Desi and Kass the following weekend.

"You're invited to that, of course," she said, glancing sideways at me.

"I am?"

"Oliver is eager to use his new outdoor kitchen, and you know Kass. She's more comfortable at home, anyway."

"They bought a house together?" I knew the night of the Oscars that Kassi and Oliver would reconcile, probably with his brother Theo as part of the deal. Kass was the last person I'd expect to be part of a threesome, but I'd seen the trio on set. They fit together perfectly.

"Sorry, I thought you knew. Yeah, they bought an old ranch. It's perfect. No neighbors for miles. I've been hearing remodeling stories for months. When Desi redid her house, she would show us paint swatches and such, but she was doing it alone. Kassi has two other people to consider and apparently, they all have pretty strong opinions."

"And yet..." I prompted, though I had a feeling about what came next.

"And yet, I've never seen her so happy," Sami said.

Oliver had been on the road for years, living out of a suitcase for the most part. He struck me as someone needing the anchor of a home base, which was one of the reasons his youngest brother accompanied him on set. Theo, artistic and withdrawn, was like Kassi, looking for a place to belong. "It sounds like exactly what they needed," I said.

"You're pretty good at reading people," Sami said, studying me through narrowed eyes.

"It's what I do," I said with a shrug. I had to figure out what everyone on set needed to do their best work. With everyone, not just the actors, I needed to understand how much direction was too much, so I didn't stifle their creativity or leave them rudderless and on their own.

Chapter Twenty-Nine

JARROD

One convenient thing about Carmen being so young, I discovered, was that she took naps. That meant Sami and I could take a "nap" too. We left music on in Carmen's room and turned on the television in Sami's. I teased Sami until she clamped her hands over her mouth to keep from making a sound. The high, squeaking noises that escaped sent the blood rushing straight to my cock. Personally, I'd never enjoyed vanilla sex more.

I finally persuaded her to come out to dinner in the middle of the week. That meant talking Lucia into taking Carmen for the evening in addition to most of the day, which apparently took more bargaining than it had in the past.

Lucia answered the door when I knocked. I felt like a teenager taking his girlfriend out on a date, especially when Lucia had me wait in the foyer while she went to get Sami.

Carmen and Maia came running.

"Hi, Jarrod!" Carmen said.

"Arrgh, it be the Captain," Maia said before bursting into giggles.

"I need to find a proper Captain's hat," I said.

"Get one with a big feather," Maia said.

"A peacock feather," Carmen agreed.

"I'll look for that," I said. But a sound drew my attention away. I'd seen pictures of Sami dressed up for red carpets and other events, but as usual, pictures didn't compare to reality. She wore a green cocktail dress that hugged and highlighted her curves. Her dark curly hair hung loose. She'd worn it down more often than not lately. I loved that she was relaxed enough around me to be natural instead of wound tight.

"Mommy, you look so pretty," Carmen said.

"Thank you, baby," Sami said.

"Can we have popcorn now?" Maia asked.

"We'll make some when we get home," Lucia said. She gave me a once over and nodded her approval. "Have a good night."

"You too."

Sami hugged Carmen goodbye, and we all trooped out of the house. Sami locked the door, and we watched Lucia walk with the two little girls. The path between the houses was well lit. Carmen and Maia ran ahead, laughing the whole time.

"You look so beautiful," I said.

Sami smiled. "You're not so bad yourself." She laid her hand on my lapel. I'd dressed up too. "You know, we could forget about dinner and go back in the house instead."

I brushed my lips up her jawline to the shell of her ear. "But all the toys are at my house."

She shivered. "Well, in that case..."

Dinner was torture. I didn't taste my food and couldn't focus on conversation. I wasn't one for mixing food and sex, but watching Sami eat was killing me. She must have known, because she slowed down and wrapped her lips sensually around a bite of salmon. I looked down at my plate. What had I even ordered? Some sort of chicken. I might as well get it wrapped up and hand it to a homeless person.

"I'm guessing you don't want dessert," Sami said, laughter in her voice.

"Only if you do."

Her eyes dropped, and she lifted her chin like she was looking over the edge of the table. "What I want isn't on the menu."

I waved down our server and threw cash at the check. My brain couldn't calculate numbers right then. There was enough to pay the bill twice over and I didn't care in the slightest. Waiting for the valet to get my car was an ordeal. Worse when I realized I'd left all my cash on the table. Sami laughed and tipped the valet. He seemed pleased with the result.

"I parked cars to pay for college," Sami said. "It was better than waiting tables."

I managed to make some sound of acknowledgment. As much as I loved that dress she was wearing, I couldn't wait to get her out of it.

Chapter Thirty

SAMI

I finally got to see the leather cuffs Jarrod had
mentioned. They were soft and the other end
attached somewhere on his bed. I'd tried to see the arrange-
ment, but he was too eager to get me exactly where I was,
bound and spread out before him. The way he looked at me
went straight to my head like the strongest alcohol. I could have
felt vulnerable, naked as I was, but he stared like he wanted me
more than his next breath. I was the one with the power here.

He'd shown me the release on the cuffs as he bound my
wrists and had me try it, so I knew I could free myself if I
wanted.

"I was in a stage production of *Gerald's Game*," he
explained.

I had so many responses to that, but they disappeared
when he brought out the toys. The first was a riding crop that
ended with soft fur on one side and leather on the other. He
stroked the fur between my breasts and over my nipples. I
squirmed and arched to his touch. He flipped the crop and
tapped the underside of one breast before soothing away any

sting with the fur again. I moaned, definitely not in pain. "You're such a tease."

He kept that up, the building pleasure with tiny interruptions of sharpness that barely qualified as pain and just pushed me higher. When his tongue finally touched my clit, I blew apart. He used the quick release to get me out of the cuffs, but when I reached for him, he pushed me back on the bed. "I've only just started to play."

The man loved his toys. They were new. I was pleased to see that. He opened plastic wrapping and stepped into the bathroom to wash them before coming back to me. A vibrator nearly made me float off the bed because my clit was already so swollen and over sensitive. I rolled away to catch my breath, and he took the chance to get a pillow under my hips. I wiggled my ass. I wanted him to spank me, but he spread my cheeks and circled that tight spot with his finger instead.

"What about this?"

I sighed and pushed back into him. "What about it?"

"Interested?"

"Hell, yes. I want you inside me."

Something cold hit me there. Lube. Of course, he had lube at the ready. Then he was teasing me, slowly breaching that tight ring, but it was something fairly slender and made of rubber.

"No," I whined. "I want you, not a toy."

"Hush." He smacked my ass. I grinned and leaned back into him. He smacked the other side. "What am I going to do with you?"

"Fuck me," I said. "Duh."

He did, but with the toy. I moaned, though it wasn't much of a protest. He finished playing and left it fully in me. I looked back to see what he was doing.

"A remote? Seriously? Men and their... Oh god." The toy moved and flexed inside me.

"You were saying?" he asked, leaning over me to kiss the back of my neck and down my spine.

"I-I was..." Rational thought had burned away. My sanity couldn't be too far behind. "Jarrod, please, you're killing me."

I heard a condom wrapper and almost sobbed with relief. He entered me in one hard thrust. My hands scrabbled on the mattress, searching for something, anything, to grip. I needed to anchor myself before I floated away on an ocean of sensation.

Jarrod gripped my hair and pulled me up so my back was against his chest. Even then, he was careful to get enough and support me with his hand so it didn't hurt enough to dim my pleasure. He kept thrusting, and I could only arch my back to help him get the perfect angle.

"I can't get enough of you," he panted into my ear. "You're all I can think about. I'm losing my fucking mind, Sam."

"Join the club."

He produced the vibrator out of nowhere and clicked it up to full speed.

"Oh, no, don't you dare." He put it on my clit and I shrieked, any bit of self-control long gone. I might have blacked out, or my brain short circuited. I was vaguely aware of Jarrod removing the toys and gently sliding into me again. I was facing him then, which was good. That was what I wanted, to look into his dark eyes and watch his face as he lost control. I wrapped myself around him and held on tight.

"I can't get enough of you either," I said into his ear.

He pulled back enough to look at me. His thrusts became erratic, wild. He had one hand on the bed to hold his weight, the other cupped my face. "Sami, I..."

His eyelids fluttered. I felt his muscles go tight and then relax. He fell next to me. I kissed his damp forehead, held his face to my chest and stroked his damp hair. He clung to me even as his muscles shook from exhaustion. "Stay with me," he said.

"Yes," I answered and assured myself that he was just talking about that night.

Chapter Thirty-One

JARROD

*K*assi was laughing when she opened the door. She seemed so different from the first time I met her. She would always be shy, but in this space at least, she appeared comfortable and at peace. She wore a long dress that suited her nicely. Her blue-green eyes sparkled.

"Welcome to the castle," she said and knelt to address Carmen. "Theo is waiting for you, birthday girl. Straight out there." She pointed to the glass doors at the back of the house. Carmen's feet echoed on the tile floor as she ran into the backyard. We watched Theo pretend to be a monster and chase her around.

"She'll sleep tonight," Kassi promised. "In the meantime, I'll give you the tour."

It wasn't a castle. Oliver would never live in anything as ostentatious as that. We were opposites that way. The house was an old ranch with thick adobe walls and minimalist decoration. Kassi showed us her office, lined with bookshelves, a desk by the window and furniture comfortable enough in appearance that it all but beckoned anyone looking to come in and curl up with a book. Theo had claimed a long, narrow room that had probably been a porch and was now lined with windows. Numerous easels stood sentry, some with cloths over them. A large piece of plywood protected the wall. An oversized canvas hung on that I could see the staples keeping it in place.

"That's interesting," I said. The lines and swirls had a distinctively feminine look to them.

Kassi and Sami shared a look. Their shoulders shook with suppressed laughter.

"What?" I asked, though looking at the canvas, I could imagine where Theo had copied those particular curves. "Kass, are you blushing?"

She covered her face with her hands. "Moving on."

I caught Sami's hand as we walked. I could see Oliver's touch in the game room and bar and the fitness room beyond that. The kitchen was large and modern, but homey at the same time in a way that the minimalist decorations elsewhere were not.

"Kass, I love this," Sami said.

Kassi shrugged. "They cook more than I do, but I knew how a kitchen should look. The dining room is me too. I told Oliver that if he wanted ultra-modern, he chose the wrong house."

Personally, I thought they chose the perfect house. The nearest neighbor was far enough away that only the lights from their house could be seen in the darkness. Despite the glow of light pollution in the distance, it was dark enough for star gazing. The back patio was private by design, a large space with an outdoor kitchen, fire pit and dining area.

"Wait," Sami teased. "Is that a television? Surely not. I remember someone mocking me for having a television on my veranda. What was it you said? Something about getting away from glowing screens and appreciating the great outdoors?"

Kassi sighed. "Life is about compromise," she said primly. "Also, it was this or listen to them shout at the soccer game while I was trying to work."

"It's called *fotboll*," Oliver said, catching Kassi around her waist and pulling her back against him. "And you'd better learn to like it. We'll be going to games next time we go home."

"Lots of drunk and screaming Europeans," Kassi said. "Yay."

Desi appeared. "You must be talking about soccer."

"*Fotboll*!" Theo and Oliver said at the same time.

"Soccer!" Carmen insisted and burst into giggles when Oliver picked her up and made her fly like a superhero to the seating area.

"I call it football too," Patrick said when Oliver set Carmen down.

"If it's football, why don't they wear helmets?" Carmen demanded.

Patrick looked to Theo for help. Theo shrugged.

"She's got you there," I laughed.

Carmen grinned and came to sit next to me.

"How was Ireland?" Sami asked.

"Great," Desi said with a hint of sarcasm. "I could barely understand a word anyone said. Now I know how Kassi feels." She poked Oliver's arm. "Apparently, I nearly caused Great Aunt Gertrude to have a heart attack."

"What happened?" Sami asked.

"She asked when we were getting married."

Sami and Kassi both gasped.

"Right," Desi said. "Now imagine that same reaction in a woman who is around a hundred and five."

"Why? What did you tell her?" Kassi asked. Her eyes were wide.

"I said I don't believe in marriage."

"The collective gasp of horror nearly made the entire building collapse into a black hole," Patrick said. He grinned mischievously and kissed Desi's ear. Dimples appeared in his cheeks. "You could have shouted 'God save the queen' and gotten a similar reaction."

"I'll remember that for next time," Desi said.

"Great Aunt Gertrude is very Catholic," Patrick explained. "Des won her over later, though. Ask me how."

Desi groaned.

"How did she win them over, Patrick?" I asked. If I sounded gleeful, it's because I was. Desi was like the little sister I never had. Teasing her had become a favorite hobby.

"Funny you should ask, Jarrod," Patrick said, turning up the brogue and looking fondly at Des, who covered her face. "Kassi, would it be all right if I commandeer your television?"

"Not my television," Kassi said, shaking her head.

It took a moment for Theo to find the remote and allow Patrick's phone to connect with the television. Once it did, there was Desi, playing the violin with three others while everyone around them clapped in time to the music.

"I knew you played the fiddle!" I teased. Sami elbowed my ribs. "Ouch!" I said.

"I had to do something," Desi said. "Great Aunt Gertrude was getting ready to douse me with holy water."

"I like that music," Carmen declared.

"You could learn to dance to it," Patrick suggested.

"Oh, I can just see that, a little Latina in the *Riverdance* ensemble," Sami quipped.

"What does that mean?" Carmen asked.

"It means I'll be the one showing you the dance steps," Patrick said.

"That's a great idea," Desi said. She picked up Patrick's phone and got the offensive video off the screen.

Chapter Thirty-Two

SAMI

"I bet you guys haven't seen Sami's birthday party on set," Jarrod said.

"I heard about it," Theo said.

Jarrod took control of the large screen.

Oliver leaned over to say close to Kassi's ear, "See? I told you we needed the television."

She pushed him away, which only put her closer to Theo, who had taken the spot on her other side. "I'd like to point out how inconvenient a smaller screen would have been," Theo said.

"I give up!" she said, casting her eyes heavenward, but she snuggled under Oliver's arm and laced her fingers with Theo's.

I appeared on the screen. "Are you filming me? Stop it. That's weird."

"Mommy, you're on TV," Carmen said. She climbed onto Jarrod's lap and giggled when she saw him on screen. "That's Jarrod," she told everyone. "Mommy, were you really scared of Jarrod?"

"Your mommy is scared of every clown," Desi said.

I gave her my best "I am not amused" look, to which she was completely immune.

Carmen found all this very funny. She didn't find it so funny when Jarrod pretended to break my neck at the end. She turned to frown at him, as full of outrage as a four-year-old child could be. He pointed to the screen. "It was just pretend. Watch."

The editing department had added full credits over the song, "Everybody Loves a Clown." They ended with an extra scene, me looking at the camera as I walked away from Jarrod. "He is one creepy motherfucker," she said.

"Creepy motherfucker," Carmen repeated.

I groaned. Carmen already knew her share of curse words. She spent a lot of times with adults and remembered everything. According to Lucia, Carmen had even taught Maia a few new phrases.

Kassi swooped in to the rescue. "That's a grown up word. Remember we talked about those?"

Carmen nodded solemnly.

"Remember the only one you're allowed to say?"

Carmen thought for a minute. "Pay-tree-arc-all bullshit!" she proclaimed.

Desi and Kass applauded.

"When she says that in school, I'm going to send you two in for the parent teacher conference," I threatened.

"Worth it," Desi said.

"Definitely," Kass agreed.

"What's this?" Sami asked as the video continued.

"Just some outtakes from the week," Jarrod said.

On the screen, Desi danced around to "Hey Mickey" while Mickey stood, tall, austere and disapproving.

"You are ridiculous," Mickey said.

"But you love me anyway," Des said and kept dancing. "Right?"

"Hmmm," Mickey said.

Desi sighed and walked away, looking forlorn. The moment her back was turned, Mickey glanced at the camera and showed off some excellent moves. Someone cheered and Desi looked back. The moment she did, Mickey resumed their stiff posture and stern expression.

Carmen thought this was great. "Mickey is just like Baby Groot," she said, which sparked a discussion of Marvel films.

Theo kissed Kassi behind her ear. "I should get the salad ready."

"I need to check the grill," Oliver said.

"I think I saw a present for a certain birthday girl around here," Patrick said.

"I'm a birthday girl!" Carmen said, bouncing off Jarrod's lap and running over to Patrick and Desi.

Patrick produced a large, brightly wrapped box, which Carmen was more than happy to rip open. Desi left them to it. "You brought it out, so you get to help her build it." She went over to sit next to Kassi.

"Cool!" Carmen said. "Mommy, look!"

It was a dinosaur robot construction set. Once it was together, she could use a controller to make it move. The toy was a bit advanced for a four-year-old, but Carmen liked building toys, and she liked to see how things worked. "Are you going to help?" I asked Jarrod. I could tell he was itching to get the box open. He and Carmen had constructed a complete Lego city in the den. I'd only been allowed to participate in the car chases through the "streets" and even then, was not allowed to deviate from the story they'd created. Jarrod grinned like a little boy and joined Patrick and Carmen at the large tiled table. I joined Kassi and Desi.

"So they both cook?" Desi was saying. "How did you manage that?"

Kassi shrugged. "To be fair, they both like to eat way

more often than I do. If it was left to me, they'd both starve. Oliver is Mr. Health Food and Theo isn't far off. Doesn't Patrick cook?"

"Patrick's version of cooking dinner is choosing where to order take out," Desi said. "What about Jarrod? I can't picture him cooking."

"He makes some pretty fantastic waffles," I said.

They shared a look.

"Knock it off," I said, glancing over to the table where Patrick and Carmen were sorting the pieces while Jarrod studied the instructions.

"Carmen likes him," Desi said. She studied her fingernails like the polish held the secrets of the universe.

"Carmen likes lots of people," I said, but I could see her getting attached to Jarrod. It was a serious problem. "He'll be on location in Taiwan soon," I said. My stomach twisted as I said it. "And we'll be in Germany. She'll be so busy learning new things that she'll forget all about him."

"You think so?" Kassi asked. There was no edge to her question, just concern.

"What about you?" Desi asked. Her gray eyes told me that she wasn't buying my nonsense. "Are you going to 'forget all about him'?"

"Don't make it into more than it is," I said.

Kassi's forehead wrinkled as her eyebrows drew together.

"Denial ain't just a river in Egypt," Desi said.

She wore that "I'm right, and you know it" smirk. I wanted to say something snarky to make it go away. I hated that particular expression, more so because she usually *was* right.

Chapter Thirty-Three

JARROD

*W*e made some good progress with the robot, but were nowhere near finished when Theo appeared with the appetizers and salad. Oliver seemed pleased with the progress of the main dish. He opened bottles of wine and champagne. Carmen got her own glass of sparkling cider, which pleased her greatly. She was less thrilled with the stuffed mushrooms and salad.

"There's a fungus among us!" Patrick said.

Theo slid a plate in front of Carmen. "Don't worry, *flicka*, I made something just for you."

Carmen studied the offering. "Are they taquitos?"

"Kind of," Theo said.

"More like a cheese stick," Kassi said.

Carmen tried once and pronounced them excellent. Between courses, Theo fired up his pizza oven and had Carmen help with the preparation. It only took a few minutes, but she had a cheese pizza while the rest of us ate grilled vegetables, steak, and salmon. Everyone was able to relax and enjoy. Carmen joined right in with the dinner conversation. I could see why she was so articulate. She was around adults more than other children.

We ate and reveled in each other's company. I'd never been in a relationship long enough to hang out with other couples. It was strangely enjoyable. Patrick and I were friends from way back, and I knew Oliver and Theo from when we'd made Kassi's film. Seeing them in their own space away from the set was surprisingly humanizing. I worked hard, but Oliver's focus put me to shame, and I had an idea Kassi was even more driven. I found them a little intimidating, if I was honest. Theo managed to soften them both. He exuded ease and relaxation, like a house cat. When Carmen started to fade, he spoke softly into Kassi's ear. They both looked at Sami and me.

"How 'bout we have Carmen sleep over tonight?" Kassi asked Sami softly.

Not softly enough though, because Carmen perked right up. "A sleepover? Can I, Mommy? Please?"

"What are you up to?" Sami asked.

"She's getting tired, and you two look like you're ready for bed," Kassi gave me a knowing look. "We have a guest room and plenty of Anime to watch. Oliver has been wanting to try a new chocolate chip pancake recipe."

Kassi, apparently, loved her Anime. She got Carmen into it and had the little girl watching for story beats and character arcs. I knew this because Carmen had explained several of them to me. Desi and Kass both enjoyed influencing Sami's daughter. Desi took the musical side and Kassi the storytelling. What was left for me? I wondered. She enjoyed building things. I could teach her about set construction, but Sami could do that just as easily. I wanted them to need me, just a little.

"She needs to brush her teeth," Sami said.

"I have extra toothbrushes," Kassi said.

"Yay!" said Carmen.

"I think that's our cue," Desi tugged Patrick's arm.

"I owe you one," I said as I passed Kassi. I adored Carmen, but I wanted a night alone with her mother.

Chapter Thirty-Four

SAMI

"You planned this," I said, glancing briefly at Jarrod as I drove home. "You conspired with my friends."

"Can't they be my friends too?"

"Desi already is, but you can't have Kass. She's mine."

"Okay." He laughed. "Hmmm, what should we do with your house all to ourselves? Unless you'd rather go back to my place?"

"No, we'll stay at my house."

"You don't like my house?" Why did he sound so concerned?

"Your house is fine. It's just—"

"Just what?"

"Remember when I called you domineering?"

He turned as much as his seatbelt would allow. "You meant that?"

"Not precisely, I meant..." I scowled at the road ahead of me. "You're always in control when we play."

"That's not true," he objected. "I might be the one with the toys, but you are always in control. Don't you know that?"

I thought about how powerful I felt, even when my hands were cuffed to his headboard. "Yes, but... I want to be the one in actual control."

"You want to dominate me."

I glanced at him again. "Yes."

He settled back in his seat. "Okay."

"What?"

"I said okay."

He'd said before that he would kneel at my feet, but I didn't believe him. "Have you ever done this before?" I asked, a little afraid of the answer.

"No, but I'll try it. What the hell?"

"What the hell?" I mimicked him. "Like it's nothing. Is everything really that easy for you?"

"No, I just don't waste time worrying."

Was that a dig? I over thought everything. Given the way Jarrod planned every part of his productions, I'd assumed he did the same.

"Besides," he continued. "What's the worst that can happen? If you do something I don't like, I'll tell you to stop and you'll stop."

I glanced at him before turning my gaze back on the road. Was it really that easy for him? Did he really not care about the power exchange or putting himself in someone else's hands? I felt a flash of fear. Was he that shallow, that his feelings all stayed on the surface and nothing actually touched him inside?

"Hey." His hand landed on my thigh and squeezed briefly. "I trust you, okay? And you're hot when you're all powerful and in control."

That wicked grin was going to be the death of me.

And so we ended up in my bedroom.

"You sure about this?" I asked. I couldn't believe he'd just hand me control like this.

"I'll do anything you want," Jarrod said. "You must know that by now."

His dark eyes looked almost black in the dim light. I'd kept the lights down and lit some candles for ambience. We'd see what "anything you want" really meant. I went to the closet and found my yoga mat. Doubling it over, I put in on the hardwood floor. "Alright then, strip and kneel there."

"Yes, Mistress," he said.

Jarrod shed his clothes quickly and knelt on the mat, his arms folded behind his back, his head down. I circled him, appreciating his fit form, the high, tight roundness of his buttocks.

"Look at me," I said. "Whenever I'm in front of you, I want to see those big brown eyes."

"Yes, Mistress." He looked up at me, his eyes soft and worshipful. He stared at me like he was a peasant and I was his queen. I wore a lace teddy that was so short it barely grazed the top of my thighs. He could see my matching panties any time I moved.

I studied him, the dark hair sprinkled across his chest and lower, forming that dark line leading to his groin. His cock wasn't fully erect, but it wasn't soft either. Some part of this, kneeling before me, being completely at my mercy or just being naked, turned him on. I didn't think I'd ever seen his face so open. I stroked his cheek. "Look at you, all sweet and submissive. I didn't know you had it in you."

He didn't say anything, waiting for my permission to speak. I didn't grant it. I liked him like this.

"So what shall I do with you?" I asked, this time running my hand down his spine to cup his ass. He shivered at my touch. "Should I spank this pretty ass?" I gave him a firm smack. He gasped. His cock jumped. "I think you might like that." I ran the nails of my left hand over the top of his thighs, never getting too close. "You can't hide from me," I crooned in his ear. "You have a lie detector right here that tells me if you like what I'm doing or if you don't." I gave him a squeeze. He moaned. With my right hand, I teased the crack of his ass. "What about back here? What else should I do?" I probed until I found his tight little bud.

Jarrod looked at me over his shoulder, his eyes wide, but in my left hand, his cock gave another little jump.

"Has no one ever touched you here?" I asked, all the while gently probing with my fingers.

"No, Mistress," he said, barely above a whisper.

"Would you like it if I did?" I pressed on that tight ring of muscles, just penetrating the tiniest bit. His cock went rock hard in my hand. "Don't bother to answer. Your body already spoke for you."

His expression was one of trepidation mixed with desire and submission. Is that how I looked when he was in control? No wonder he got off on it. This sort of power was a heady thing. I could get used to it. I stroked his hair and drew his head down against my shoulder. "Don't worry. I'll only use a little plug. It won't hurt, and you always have your safe word. Understand?"

"Yes, Mistress," he said, leaning into me like he needed my comfort. Was this the same Jarrod Colosi, or had he been replaced with a body double? I drew away to study his face. Gone was the smart ass twinkle in his eyes, that sardonic smile. He was completely at my mercy. He really did trust me, I realized. How and when did that happen? I wasn't sure I was worthy.

"Get up," I commanded. "Bend over the bed, ass in the air."

He complied quickly. "Stay there," I said and went to my toy cabinet. I'd bought some supplies since we started playing together. I found the plug I had in mind. It was fairly slim and not terribly long. Perfect to start. Lube was necessary, of course. I wanted the pleasure of warming his backside with my hand, but I brought out a small paddle too, and of course, the restraints. I would tie Jarrod up and tease him until he was as desperate and needy as he made me.

I returned and paused for a moment to appreciate him in that position. He jumped when I laid my hand on his lower cheek. "All that running you do is worth every minute," I said, smoothing my hand over his skin. "You have a beautiful ass." I slapped him. He moaned softly. I slapped the other side in an upward motion, catching the underside where he sat. "So nice and tight," I squeezed him. "Looks great in jeans, but you know that, don't you?" I spanked him in even, moderate strokes. He actually arched as if asking for more. I had done that too.

"You like this?" I asked. I brought my hand down hard. "Answer me."

"Yes, Mistress," he gasped.

"Yes, what?"

"Yes, I like it."

"For someone who demands such precise communication from others, you sure are being vague." I delivered several hard smacks to his sit spots. They were turning a lovely shade of pink. "Care to try again?"

"I like it when you spank me, Mistress!"

"That's better." I smoothed away the sting. "Let's see what else you like." I climbed onto the center of the bed, so my back was against the headboard. "Get over her. Lie across my lap." The plug, lube and paddle were all within reach on the nightstand. If Jarrod noticed them, he made no comment, but just complied with my orders. I felt his rock hard erection against my thigh. I wanted that inside me, but he needed a bit more attention first. I stroked his back and felt the tremors going through him. "Nervous?" I asked.

"A little," he confessed.

"Spread your legs."

He did, and I reached down to stroke his balls gently. He moaned. I spread his cheeks and dropped a dollop of lube on his tight hole. He flinched. "Relax," I soothed, rubbing circles on his back. "I won't hurt you like that, only in a good way, promise."

I opened the wrapper on the plug and circled his tight bud with the tip. His muscles tensed so tight, he was shaking. "Jarrod," I said, "relax."

He tried to, I could tell by watching, but the moment the plug got close, he tensed again.

"You can safe word out. You know that," I reminded him.

"Yes, Mistress," he said through what sounded like clenched teeth, but he didn't say it.

"Relax. It will hurt if you don't."

"I-I don't think I can," he admitted.

"I could paddle your ass until you relax," I threatened. "Is that what you want?"

He was breathing hard now. "Yes," he gasped.

"I'm sorry, what?"

"That's what I want. I want you to paddle me."

If I couldn't feel his cock throbbing against my leg, I might have hesitated, but he really did want this. Was it so strange? Hadn't I responded the same way when he showed me a paddle the first time?

I picked up the paddle and covered his rounded ass in quick, sharp smacks. He strained towards the contact. I paddled him harder, turning his beautiful ass red. He tensed and squirmed and finally fell limp across my lap. He'd come a little from the spanking. I felt the wet spot on my leg. I dropped the paddle and soothed his hot skin, leaning down to kiss him and press my face into all that heat. He moaned. I lubed up the plug and squirted more directly onto him. He didn't fight me this time. I spread his cheeks with one hand

and slowly, carefully breached his tight hole with the tip of the plug. I pushed it in and withdrew, pushed it a bit further and withdrew again.

"What are you doing?" he gasped. "I thought you were just going to put it in."

"I'm fucking you with it," I answered calmly. "You enjoy fucking me with every toy you can. How does it feel?"

"I don't know. Weird."

"Does it hurt?"

"No, not now."

"Good. It gets a little wider at the base, but once it's completely inside you, you're going to sit on a hard chair while I ride your cock. Every time you thrust into me, you'll feel the plug in your ass, and of course, it'll make you aware of your sore backside, too. That's a bonus."

He groaned at my words, but it didn't sound like a complaint. I pushed the plug all the way to the flared section and paused, letting it stretch him. His hands gripped the edge of the mattress so hard his knuckles turned white. I moved the plug around a bit and he pressed his face into the bed, muttering.

"Care to say that a little louder?" I asked, still teasing him with the plug.

"Please," he gasped. "You're killing me, please."

"Please what?"

"I need to come, please let me fuck you."

"But I'm busy fucking *you*," I teased, almost withdrawing the plug completely before pushing it all the way in. He groaned loudly. I pushed all the way to the base this time. His tight ring of muscle clamped on the small part before the wide base. I tapped the base a few times, enjoying the shivers that went through him when I did.

"Please," he gasped again.

"Okay, stand up."

He did, somewhat awkwardly, as he tried to adjust to the invasion. His cock was hard and quivering, dark and engorged with blood. I thought about sucking him off to give him some relief, but this was all about pushing limits, wasn't it?

"Stand there and wait," I said. I felt his eyes follow me out of the room now, no longer soft and submissive. Jarrod's dark gaze was full of lust. I marveled that he could hold back and do as I commanded. I returned with a kitchen chair. I'd removed the cushion and left the hard, wood seat bare. "Sit," I said.

He did, flinching a little when his sore backside made contact, then again when the plug pushed deeper into him.

"Hold onto the back," I said. "You're not allowed to touch me."

He raised tortured dark eyes to meet mine, but did as he was told.

I straddled his lap, but just grazed his cock. My panties were soaked through. There was no denying that. "Is your ass sore?" I breathed the question close to his ear.

"Yes, Mistress."

"Does it feel good?"

"Yes, Mistress."

I gripped his cock and rubbed the head against the wet lace of my panties. The friction had to be torture. He moaned.

"Is this what you want?"

"Yes," he groaned through his teeth.

"And you think you deserve it?"

"Please, Sami," he begged.

"What did you call me?"

"I-I, oh fuck, please, I can't take this."

"I'm sure you can," I said. The pressure of his cock head rubbing the lace against my clit was making me crazy, too. "But you've been so good that I won't tease you anymore."

He sighed with relief.

"For now anyway."

He jerked his head up to look at me, but I took that moment to push my panties aside and slide down onto him. His hips started at once, grinding and thrusting into me. I rose and fell, increasing the impact of his thrusts.

"How does that plug feel?" I asked.

"I want to touch you," he said instead of answering. "Please, let me touch you, Mistress."

I drew his face down to my breasts and let him touch me that way. His mouth latched onto one of my nipples through the lace of the teddy. It was my turn to cry out. He moved to the other, leaving wet lace behind. The cool air made my areola tighten even more. I plunged my hands into his hair, trying to pull him closer. His fingers dug into my hips. He'd let go of the chair and now he took control without my permission. I didn't complain, because he changed the angle and managed to hit that sensitive spot deep inside me.

"Sami," he gasped against my skin. "I can't last much longer. Come first. Please, come for me."

I pressed him back against my breast. He sucked the oversensitive peak into his mouth. I guided one of his hands to my clit. He found it with his thumb and rubbed furiously until I flew apart in his arms. He kept thrusting, holding me tight and pushing into me with no sense of control or restraint. His gasps had become moans and now they changed to shouts. I felt him jerk inside me as he came, his face pressed into my neck. I held him as he shuddered his release and clung to me until he could move again.

"I've never felt anything like that," he said finally, his dark eyes held amazement. I kissed him deeply, not ready yet for this to end.

"Take a minute if you need to, then I want you on the bed," I said and slid off of him.

"The plug?" he asked, his voice small and shy. This was a totally different side of Jarrod Colosi.

"Leave it," I said.

His eyebrows drew down, but he didn't complain. He padded off to the bathroom and shut the door. I used the time to tie restraints around the bedposts. The cuffs were soft nylon. They wouldn't leave a mark unless he really put up a fight. I smiled to myself. I planned on tormenting enough that he would struggle against the bonds, but not enough to hurt his tender skin.

"When did you get those?" Jarrod asked from behind me.

I'd been so intent on the cuffs, that I didn't hear him come out. "Just the other day," I answered lightly. "On the bed with you."

His dark eyes darted from the bed to me and back again, but he complied. I gripped his legs and moved him as I wanted, securing one ankle and then the other until they were spread wide.

"Arms up," I said. He allowed me to cuff one wrist and watched me closely while I leaned over him to cuff the other. "Comfy?"

"I'm alright."

"Good. I'll be right back."

"Sami!" He cried in protest.

"I'm just going to clean up. Five minutes tops. You lie there and relax. Be good and I'll let you come again. Be naughty and..." I tapped my lips with my finger. "I think I have nipple clamps around here somewhere."

"Oh, fuck no!"

"I'm sorry, did you forget who is dominating whom? You can use your safe word if you must, but otherwise, you will behave yourself, or deal with the consequences. Understand?"

"Yes, Mistress," he said, full of contrition.

"That's better. Now, I will be right back." I permitted

myself a long slow look at his body before I went into the bathroom and closed the door behind me. He was half erect as I left him.

I knew I wouldn't like being left alone, naked and tied up, so I didn't leave Jarrod for long, either. I discarded the lace panties, soaked with more than my fluids now, and returned wearing only the lace teddy. I could feel Jarrod's eyes on me like a touch.

I got a few more toys out of the cabinet and put them within reach. He craned his neck to see what I was doing. I kissed him to stop his questing gaze. He moaned when my tongue parted his lips. He opened willingly to me and protested when I pulled away. One of these nights, I was going to spend an hour just kissing him. In the meantime, though, I was going to have some fun. I sucked on his earlobe and smiled when he shivered.

"I want you again," he gasped.

"Do you?" I lifted my ass and peered down between us to where his cock stood, hard and eager. "I guess you do. You'll have to wait, though. Last time was entirely too quick for my tastes. This time, we're going slow. You're going to learn patience."

I pinched both his nipples at the same time. He bucked under me, not like he was in pain. I kissed them to ease any remaining sting and sucked gently at the sensitive peaks. He moaned. The taut muscles in his stomach flinched as I trailed my fingernails over them. My mouth followed, learning every ridge and valley. He tried to thrust his hips. I ignored him and knelt between his knees. His hips seemed to move of their own accord, jutting his cock at me, begging for attention. Every movement would make him feel the plug. I could see it affecting him. His breathing came in short, rough gasps.

"Please, Sami," he moaned.

"What did you say?" I demanded. My fingernails were on his inner thighs, closing in on his balls.

"I mean, please, Mistress."

"That's better." I teased the plug, and he whimpered. "I think you like this toy," I said, teasing that sensitive spot just under his balls and pushing at the edge of the plug base to change the angle. "Do you like having a plug in your ass, Jarrod?"

He made that desperate sound again.

"I asked you a question." My fingers stilled on his skin.

"Yes, I like it," he groaned.

"Good boy." I ran my nails over his balls and along the underside of his cock. He shuddered at my touch. "so responsive," I crooned. "You're much more present when you can't move."

"Please," he cried.

"Please what?" I asked innocently.

"Take me in your mouth."

I slid my hand up one side of him, swirled it over the crown of his cock, and down the other side. "Now, I do believe that is what they call 'topping from the bottom.' And I will have none of it. I'd punish your pretty ass, but we've already done that today." My fingers slid over his silky skin lightly, too lightly to give him what he wanted, just enough to tease. "So how should I punish you?"

He looked worried. Smart man.

Chapter Thirty-Five

JARROD

*S*ami left me shaking and exhausted mentally as well as physically. She let me bury my face where her shoulder and neck met. I inhaled her scent deeply. She stroked my hair. I loved it when she did that.

"Don't leave," I said. *Don't leave me,* is what I meant, but I'd been open and vulnerable enough for one night. I had to regain some sense of control.

"I'm not going anywhere. This is my house," Sami said. I could hear her smile in her voice. She kissed the top of my head. "Also, I'm too tired to move."

She did move, though. She turned, so I was pressed along her back, my arm around her waist, my face in those wild curls. Her breathing grew deep and even almost immediately. I held her and tried to absorb the impact of what we'd done.

I'd never allowed anyone to get that close. Being vulnerable wasn't my thing, but good god, in her capable hands, I'd come so hard, so many times. It was like nothing I'd ever imagined. I was just kidding myself if I thought it was only great sex at play. Our connection was so much deeper than that.

I had always been the one in control, the one making the decisions. It had been so relaxing, so freeing to let Sami take the reins for a while. That state of being helpless and yet still able to end everything with a word was powerful. I could see why submissives enjoyed it. I had always kept a tight rein on myself when it came to sex or anything else. Losing control, losing myself to pleasure and sensation hadn't even been in the realm of possibilities for me, until I met Sami.

I couldn't imagine the rest of my life without her. My arms tightened around her sleeping form at the mere thought. I leaned into her. I was lost, hopelessly lost in her. I kissed the top of her head and whispered something I'd never said to anyone, "I love you."

Sami was asleep and didn't hear me, but it was better, safer that way. She might not share my feelings. Maybe she would eventually. I couldn't just be some poor sap trailing after her forever. Oh, who was I kidding? Of course I could. Isn't that what I'd been doing since we met?

Chapter Thirty-Six

SAMI

I reached for Jarrod, but he wasn't there. Early morning light came through the windows. I hadn't drawn the shades last night. I'd been too distracted. That made me rise up on one elbow. Did I scare him away? It had been a power trip, no mistake there. I'd thought he'd enjoyed himself. The way he'd looked at me, his dark eyes wide and worshipful, his face open and guileless. I'd never imagined he could look that way. Maybe he hadn't either, and it had frightened him. That would probably be for the best. We were getting too close. He'd be leaving soon, and I'd go in a different direction. We each had our own worlds and while we might orbit each other for a while, the worlds couldn't collide without leaving destruction in their wake. INXS had that part wrong, no matter how pleasant their harmonies.

I braced myself for the inevitable. The voice mail or worse, text would come to tell me he had to get to work on his next project. He was leaving early. We would stay in touch, of course, but he'd be on the other side of the world for the next few months and so very busy. Eventually, we'd see each other at some awards show or other event and we'd be cordial enough. He'd have some other woman on his arm and I'd... I'd be working hard to keep all my juggling balls in the air. Carmen would miss him, but she'd find other playmates.

I showered and dressed quickly. Kassi was great with Carmen, but she'd be needing some peace and quiet soon. An evening of socializing, even with Desi and me, and then a morning with a demanding four-year-old would be too much for her.

I stopped short as I entered the kitchen. Why hadn't I noticed the coffee aroma until this moment? Was it because I didn't expect it, or because I was certain Jarrod would be gone instead of sitting at my kitchen table? He'd found the scripts for the new series. Two lay face down to the side. He was reading the third one. The rest were in another stack, awaiting his attention.

"What are you doing?"

"Shh," he said, waving me away and not bothering to look up.

"Did you just 'shh' me in my own house?" I demanded.

He looked up then, his face bright and cheerful. That cocky half grin tugged at his lips. "The coffee is brewed, goddess. I'll make breakfast in a little bit. Until then, shh." He resumed reading my script.

I huffed in a way strikingly similar to my daughter and got myself some coffee. There were no messages on my phone yet, so I wrote one to, Kassi telling her to let me know when she was ready for me to relieve her. And then there was nothing for me to do. I hated being around when someone else was reading my work for the first time. Even with Kassi and Desi, I had to be in my office instead of the writers' room for their first reading.

I could make breakfast. Jarrod was oblivious to anything I was doing, anyway. He did make excellent waffles, but he hadn't had my omelets yet.

Chapter Thirty-Seven

JARROD

My cinematic vision hadn't gone dark after all. I didn't even see the words on the page. They turned directly into images, just like they always had. I heard the characters speak instead of reading the dialogue. I could see and hear everything, and there was that part of me that stepped back and nodded approval.

The smell of eggs and peppers drew me back to reality. Sami moved the scripts aside and set a plate in front of me. She even refilled my coffee.

"I was going to cook for you," I said.

"I wanted to eat sometime this century," she said. "Hot sauce?"

"Of course," I said, taking the bottle and sprinkling it liberally on my omelet.

We ate in silence for a few moments. Sami poked at her food, chewed on her lip, and bounced her fork restlessly between her fingers. I knew what she wanted, but I waited. She watched me as I avoided looking at her. We had been playing games for years. Why should that change now? Besides, this was fun. My first day on the *Death Sucks* set, she said, *"I know it's excellent, Jarrod. I wrote it."* about her season finale. In hindsight, I recognized the bravado. Maybe she was more confident with her other two musketeers at her side, or maybe this new project was a stretch. Either way, I let her stew while I ate.

Sami huffed a sigh. Carmen did that a lot, too. "So how is it?"

I looked up. "The omelet? It's great. I can never find the right balance with eggs. Mine either end up runny or rubbery. Yours are perfect."

Her eyes narrowed.

"Oh, you meant the script," I said. I glanced at the stacks of paper on the edge of the table and shrugged. "You know, I'm just a director. I wouldn't know good writing if it bit me in the ass." She'd texted that to me while I was directing Desi's film.

"I hate you."

I smiled. "No, you don't."

She shook her head and finally began to eat.

"I do have a question."

"What's that?"

"The title," I said. "*Nevermind?* You don't strike me as a Nirvana fan."

"They're okay," she said. "My grunge taste ran more in the Pearl Jam and Soundgarden vein."

I waited for her to explain, but she just looked at me. It was another power play, but I'd started this game. I gave in first. "So why the Nirvana reference?"

"It's not a Nirvana reference. It's a Leonard Cohen reference."

I didn't know what to say to that.

"Look it up. You'll see why it fits. Now will you tell me what you think of the script?"

I wanted to find the song and listen to it, but instead, I

gave her my answer. "It's brilliant, Sam. The best thing you've written so far. You took the genre and... You didn't just flip it, you held it upside down and jostled it to get the spare change that fell out of its pockets." That was a ridiculous metaphor, but it was also incredibly accurate. She'd taken a hard-boiled detective story and twisted it, then threw in some of her signature snark, as if she was finally confident to bare her soul on the page.

She looked at me through her lashes.

"I don't suppose you need another producer?"

Those whiskey colored eyes widened. "You're going to be in Thailand."

And there it was. She didn't want me working on her project. She had her carefully constructed world, and I wasn't welcome there. "That's right," I agreed. "Silly me."

We ate in awkward silence after that. I collected the dishes over her protests. "You cooked, I'll clean. It's only fair." What wasn't fair, my inner five-year-old insisted, was that I was scheduled to work on a project that didn't inspire me at all when right there on the table was one of the best scripts I'd ever read. That story didn't put me to sleep. I had been on my second reading when Sami came out to the kitchen. The first time through, I devoured the pages, unable to read quickly enough. The second read was for savoring. I looked for the little clues, the poetry and rhythm in the dialogue. It was there, subtle but definitely present. I set the pan on the drying rack and glanced at the table again. Sami had the scripts re-stacked. Everything back in order as it had been before I pawed at it.

"I need to pick up Carmen," she said. That was all. We'd been spending the weekends together, but she didn't invite me along. I nodded. Fair enough. Her world, her rules.

"I should get going," I said. "I'll call you later." I gathered my things and kissed her goodbye. I had a script I needed to work on, after all. How could I approve locations if I didn't know what I wanted in the first place?

As I drove home, I wasn't thinking about my project. I was envisioning Sami's. Berlin was the perfect location. The architecture was modern but lacked the tall, looming buildings of New York City or London. The old world shadows still lingered, they just hid better than in other countries. War had that effect. I pulled into my driveway with little memory of how I'd gotten there. I stopped midway between the road and my house. It was barely a house at all. Oliver had gotten lost the first time he visited. He'd mistaken my house for a resort. He wasn't far off. No one person needed a house that big. I was starting to hate the place, which begged the question, why hold on to something I hated?

Chapter Thirty-Eight

JARROD

*S*ami and I texted a bit over the next few days, but didn't have any real conversations. We didn't address the space between us. I didn't know how to broach the subject. I wanted a place in her life, but she seemed to be putting distance between us instead of letting me get any closer. *"You'll be in Thailand."* I might be, but only if I didn't have any other choice.

I was standing at the proverbial crossroads, I realized. I could do what was expected and direct a summer blockbuster, or I could live for myself instead of the stereotype for a change. My house was the stereotype. The cars collecting dust in my ridiculous garage were more of the same. I didn't drive them. What was the point in having them? And there was that script in my office, the one next to the couch. Could I really get funding now? Maybe. Or I could go truly independent and fund it myself. Hell, I could even do a little acting if that was what it took. I hadn't been in front of a camera in years, but there had been offers. Other countries paid a lot for commercials starring American actors. I'd never done it. I thought it was selling out. But what was that, really? Which path would cost me my soul? Some commercials to fund the project I wanted, or the action film that didn't interest me in the slightest? I sat on my patio, a space I never actually used unless I was hosting a party, and stared out at the valley contemplating this. Beyond my career, there was the question of a home life. I didn't have one, but maybe I could if Sami would let me in.

She called me Wednesday morning. "Look, I hate to ask, but I need a favor," she said.

A favor, as in she had a meeting in Santa Monica about the new show and Lucia wasn't available. Neither was Adrianna. Desi and Kass were both out of town. That's how far down the list I was. She'd asked at least four people before calling me. I tried not to take it personally, but it stung.

I met her in Santa Monica near the pier.

Carmen took my hand and smiled up at me. "We'll be fine, Mom," she said.

Sami's eyebrows drew together. "I shouldn't be more than an hour."

"We can stay occupied until then."

Her phone chimed. Sami's frown deepened. "I have to go."

"We'll be fine." I echoed Carmen's words, as if I'd never watched Carmen before, as if I was too irresponsible or incompetent to entertain a four-year-old girl at an amusement pier on the beach.

Sami headed down the boardwalk with only one last concerned glance over her shoulder. Carmen and I waved in unison.

"Want to go on some rides?" I asked.

"Yeah!" she shouted, jumping up and down.

I bought some tickets, and we went on the Ferris wheel

first. Carmen peered out over the edge at the other rides and planned her attack.

"Bumper cars first," she said. "Then the scrambler."

Her plan changed with every rotation. I'd have to accompany her on most of the rides, but that was okay, or it was until we went on our fifth spinning ride and my head kept spinning after we got off.

"What should we go on next?"

I found some little kid rides and sent Carmen ahead on her own. "You try that one. I'm going to ride the park bench."

"How do you ride the park bench?" She stared at the bench like it was going to move somehow.

"You sit on it, of course. Go ahead and get in line. I'll be right here when you're done." I kept a close eye on Carmen as she stood in line with the other kids, and an even closer eye on the attendant who fastened the safety door on her little car. My stomach lurched when the ride started spinning. The cars lifted up and down under the riders' control, which was a thrill for little kids who never got to control much of anything. Carmen waved to me every time she went past. I narrowed my eyes to slits so I would know when to wave back.

There was a playground nearby. I convinced Carmen to give that a try after she rode the carousel. She scaled the kiddie version of a climbing wall with no problem, but didn't have the same luck with the rope walk. She kept getting up and trying again, though. The kid had spirit.

"Is that your dad?" one of the other kids asked her.

Carmen glanced at me before she answered, "Yeah."

My heart flipped. The answer came out so quickly and easily. It was a fib, but what if it became the truth? I let my imagination spin out the possibilities until Carmen lost interest in the playground and came over to me.

"I'm thirsty," she said.

"Okay, let's go get a drink. We should get a snack too. You must be hungry." The last thing I wanted to do was hand an unhappy child back to Sami.

"Okay." She took my hand and led the way to the main thoroughfare. We joined a line for french fries.

"I know you're not my daddy," Carmen explained while we waited. "I was just pretending."

I didn't know what to say to that, so I just nodded. Carmen seemed content with that and went on to recap her time on the rides and in the playground. Sami hadn't said anything about lunch one way or the other, but I knew I'd be in trouble if I gave Carmen something to spoil her appetite. So I got a small order of curly fries and a drink.

"Hey, are you Jarrod Colosi?"

"What?" I was focused on Carmen. Being recognized was the last thing I'd expected.

"You're Jarrod Colosi! I love your work. I've seen every film."

"Oh yeah? Thanks." I didn't want to ignore a fan, but Carmen was in danger of dropping her fries.

"I'm gonna sit on the bench," she said.

"Just stay where I can see you, okay?"

"Okay." I watched Carmen navigate her way across the boardwalk. She set her fries carefully on the bench before climbing up and sitting with her soda.

"I wanted to ask about..." He was a real fan. I had to give him that. He asked about technical decisions I made in a film that had been a box office failure but later became a cult classic. I stopped thinking about most of my films once I'd finished the editing process. In truth, by the final edit, I was so sick of a project, I wanted the damn thing to just go away. I did some publicity during the promotion period, but mostly left that to the talent while I moved on to the next shiny new project. There were a select few that stayed close to my heart, and he was asking about one of those.

"I would have done that, but the boom was stuck, so we had to improvise. It actually worked out better in the end." I glanced over at the bench to make sure Carmen was okay. My heart seized in my chest. The bench was empty. I left the fan mid-sentence and pushed my way through to the other side of the boardwalk. "Carmen?" I called, searching the area desperately. I didn't see her anywhere.

Was she wearing blue or purple? I couldn't remember. It had been a plain shirt, not a graphic tee. I ran into the nearest shop. "Did you see a little girl? Dark curly hair?"

The cashier shook her head. I rushed back out onto the boardwalk. She had to be around somewhere. The beach was crowded for a weekday. I couldn't see around the throngs of tourists. Two more shops with no sign of her. A candy store where they made fudge in the window drew onlookers, but not Carmen. What if someone grabbed her? Should I call the police? They could send out an Amber alert and get everyone in the area looking instead of just me. I was clearly too incompetent to do this on my own.

My chest felt like it was going to either split open or collapse in on itself. I couldn't decide which and didn't have time to worry about whether I was having a heart attack. None of that mattered. I called Carmen's name, retraced our steps to the playground, the pier. I couldn't remember where I'd looked already. Panic blinded me and froze rational thought. I'd turned into a madman. People shied away when I approached, and I could not have possibly cared any less. I jumped onto a bench to get a higher perspective. The woman sitting there clutched her bag and hurried away. I scanned the boardwalk and then the beach. Joggers and bikers passed

each other on the walk. A beach volleyball game drew specta-
tors not far from the original muscle beach equipment. No
sign of Carmen anywhere. I tried to think like a four-year-old.
Anything could have lured her away, a cute dog, a stray cat,
any one of the many street performers...

Chapter Thirty-Nine

SAMI

The meeting ran much longer than it should have. I hated studio bullshit and the corporate yahoos who talked and talked but never said anything. "First, let's agree on why we're here today," I quipped, keeping my voice down in case any of them had followed us out.

Mickey snickered next to me.

"They're so all bright eyed and ambitious," I said. They were young and determined to climb the ladder to become studio executives. "Please tell me I was never like that."

Mickey just laughed.

"Oh, come on," I said. "Was I really?"

"Not that bad," they said. "You were ambitious and determined, but never that perky. Do you think it's safe to consume that much coffee?"

"Energy drinks. That's what kids drink now. God, I'm getting old." Mickey and I had possibly been the only two people in that meeting over the age of thirty. Those kids, and they were kids, no matter how old that made me sound, said they admired me and all I had accomplished, but I saw that gleam in their eyes. They thought they would be able to get further sooner. They probably thought I was old at thirty-six, already past it, that I should get out of the way and make room for new blood.

"So Jarrod's watching the kiddo," Mickey said. "How's that going?"

"I was desperate," I said. "I need to find a nanny. One who is willing to travel." The twist in my stomach whenever I thought of moving to Germany had grown familiar by now.

"Adrianna is done with school. Did you ask her?"

"I thought she was looking for a job." I never assumed anyone was just available and waiting for my call. That kind of thinking had gotten me into trouble before.

"Only because she thinks this thing with you is temporary. Communicate, Sami. The worst that can happen is she'll say no, though I happen to know that she would love spending some time abroad."

We paused to listen to a group of musicians. It appeared to have started as a drum circle, but some acoustic guitarists had joined in. Someone played a harmonica, and someone else had an accordion. The sound was joyful, and exactly what I needed at that moment.

"Isn't that Carmen?" Mickey asked.

I spotted Carmen on the far side of the circle, her face alight with excitement. "It is," I agreed.

"I don't see Jarrod."

"Neither do I, but when I do, I'm going to disembowel him with my bare hands," I said.

Mickey caught my arm before I could barge over to where my baby stood without adult supervision. Jarrod burst through the crowd. He ran through the center of the circle, tripping over a drummer's upturned bucket and nearly falling on his face. Shit. I recognized that look of panic. It echoed deep in my chest. I'd lost Carmen before. She was too smart by half and would wander away if something interesting caught her attention.

Jarrod slid to his knees in front of my daughter. Disgruntled looks from the musicians turned to smiles. Anyone could see what had happened. Jarrod clutched Carmen's shoulders for half a moment before pulling her into a tight hug. He stood, lifting her in his arms and holding her like he would never let her go. She must have protested, because he eased up and pressed his forehead to hers. I couldn't hear him, but I could imagine what he was saying. *You scared me to death. I thought I'd lost you.* Carmen smiled and wiped at Jarrod's face. Was he crying? She kissed his cheek and wrapped her small arms around his neck. He still had both arms wrapped around her.

"Look at him," Mickey said, then gave me side eye and chuckled. "Look at *you*."

I scrubbed at my eyes. I knew Carmen was the most precious thing in the world, but was still surprised when others acted that way. Jarrod wasn't behaving like a babysitter who was angry that his charge had wandered away. He acted like he loved my daughter. His reaction was more like a parent than a regular authority figure. "It's the salt air," I said.

"Sure it is," Mickey said. "Baby girl, you're in deep. For that matter, so is he." They patted my arm. "Have fun with that. I'll see you tomorrow."

I gave Jarrod and Carmen some time to settle down before texting that I would meet them by the ice cream stand. When they arrived, I talked about my meeting and pretended nothing was out of the ordinary. *He's leaving soon*, I thought, but he had asked about producing my new series. Why would he ask that?

Chapter Forty

SAMI

*D*esi arrived at my office on Friday, bags of takeout food in hand. She came in and shut the door. I busied myself pouring drinks and making room on the small table.

"Okay, spill it," she said after maybe a minute and a half. Desi could never be accused of dancing around a subject.

"I just wanted to have lunch," I lied.

"Right. That's why we're here instead of a restaurant."

"I didn't have time to go out."

"You wanted to have a private conversation and not worry about and tabloid spies overhearing," Desi countered. "And you're feeling awkward about the topic, otherwise Kassi would be here. You didn't want us ganging up on you. Which means it concerns Jarrod."

I didn't say anything.

"Oh, stop it," she said. "If you wanted a soft touch, you would have called Kass." Desi's eyes narrowed. "Wait, you did call her first, didn't you? Should I be insulted?"

She wasn't serious. Desi knew me too well to be insulted if I called Kassi first. I had wanted a more subdued argument like I would get from her. Desi didn't bother with the kid gloves.

"What happened? Did the Vikings have her tied to the bed?"

That reminded me of Jarrod and all the things that followed after one of us was bound to the headboard. "She's on a deadline," I said.

Desi scoffed. "All of Kassi's deadlines are self-imposed for a week before the actual deadline. You didn't try very hard."

Maybe I didn't. Maybe I really did want Desi's way of seeing through my bullshit. Kassi did it too, but she would lead the conversation around in circles until I saw reality for myself.

"So what's going on?" Desi asked. "Let me guess, you agreed to move in together, and now you're having second thoughts."

"No, nothing like..." I looked at her. "Why would you say that?"

"Jarrod's house is on the market. You mean that has nothing to do with you?"

I retrieved my tablet and pulled up *Just the Buzz*. It was a gossip site that we all claimed to hate, but still used to find the latest rumors quickly.

"I didn't know," I said, staring at the article and following the link to the real estate listing. My heart throbbed like a toothache. Jarrod was giving up his ties in the area. It could only mean one thing; he was going abroad and not coming back. After Thailand, he'd go somewhere else, Canada maybe or New Zealand, spending a few months here, a few months there working on one project after another. And why not? He was a bachelor, after all. Nothing and no one waiting at home.

"Sami, breathe," Desi was saying. Her voice seemed to be coming from far away.

"He's leaving," I said. "He's leaving, and he didn't even

tell me."

"It could just be for his next project," Desi said.

"Then why sell his house? He's had it for years."

Desi shook her head. She didn't have an answer. "Call him and ask."

"I can't do that." I poked at my food, but my appetite was gone.

"Right, because refusing to talk to a man is definitely the way to go. Have you learned nothing from my example?"

I smiled because that was what Desi wanted. She had gone to Pennsylvania and then to England to avoid Patrick when they split up. He followed her. Kassi's guys had been more laid back, letting her come to them. That had been exactly the approach she needed. I couldn't see myself in either scenario. Jarrod had his eyes set on the horizon. He cared for my daughter, and probably felt something for me, but we didn't figure into his future plans. I would have to explain everything to Carmen. As much as I wanted to avoid awkward conversations, she needed a chance to say goodbye.

"What are you going to do?" Desi asked.

"I guess I'll invite him over for dinner," I said and typed out the text with my thumbs.

"Good," Desi said.

She thought I was going to have him over and hash it all out, that we would magically work it all out and live happily ever after. That might happen in her world. Mine was harsher, more grounded in reality. I'd never gotten a happy ending. Why should I expect one now?

"Talk to me." It was half request, half demand.

"He's going to leave," I said. "There's nothing keeping him here."

"Are you calling yourself nothing? Do I need to break into the song from *A Chorus Line*? I thought you didn't like it when I played Morales."

"No, I said your accent is terrible."

She conceded my point with a tilt of her head, but pressed on anyway. "Sami, he has been chasing you for over four years. He even followed the Spice Girls' advice and got with your friends in order to be your lover. Why would he walk away now?"

"Because they always do," I said. The excuses given over the years formed a cacophony of voices in my head.

You're too ambitious.

You only care about your career.

You're too intense.

Or my mother's often repeated words, *Sometimes, Samantha, you're just too much, and people need a break.*

"To be fair," Desi said, "you are basing that opinion on the actions of insecure man babies. Jarrod isn't like that."

"What if his projects tank and mine do well?" I said.

"This is the man who walked away from an incredibly successful acting career and took up residence behind the camera. You do realize that, right? If you're producing excellent content and his films flop, he'll work for you instead. He said he would."

"When did he say that?"

She thought about it. "At Carmen's birthday dinner. He said he'd be happy producing more of your shows if you would let him."

And he'd asked if *Nevermind,* my new show, needed a producer, but I couldn't assume anything. My assumptions never worked out well. "I don't believe that," I said. "He likes to be in control." Except for that time he'd knelt in front of me. The man was an enigma.

My phone beeped. "We're on for dinner," I said.

"Well then, you can try out this old fashioned notion called *communication*," Desi said.

Mickey had said something similar.

Chapter Forty-One

JARROD

*C*armen chattered through dinner. Good thing, since an invisible wall seemed to have grown between Sami and me. I had a lot to tell her, but I didn't know where to begin. I had ideas, plans, if she was willing to listen to them and provide some input, but I wasn't about to bring them up in front of Carmen. Sami could just as easily shoot my suggestions down and show me to the door. I could understand that. She'd built a world designed to suit her needs and showcase her brilliant mind.

I'd done something similar, though I had never considered myself brilliant, just hardworking and persistent. The thing was, my world had lost its appeal. My ridiculous house, for one thing, needed to go. I'd called a realtor and put it on the market. Now it was just a matter of finding a buyer, or perhaps a developer who would turn it into a spa. Hell, it was big enough to serve as an artist commune if someone wanted to pay for it. I didn't care. I'd backed out of the action film. The news wasn't out yet, and wouldn't be until everything was settled with my replacement. No one wanted the investors to panic.

"Tell Jarrod goodbye," Sami said to Carmen.

Everything inside me froze. "Goodbye" and not "Goodnight"? What did that mean?

"Bye, Jarrod," Carmen said, throwing her arms around my neck and kissing my cheek.

"Good night, sweet pea." I couldn't say goodbye. The word stuck in my throat. Sami and Carmen disappeared down the hall, and I waited in the den. I flipped through stations on the television and paced the floor. None of that was helping, so I went in the kitchen and washed the pots soaking in the sink. It was a little presumptuous, acting like I had a right to do things in the kitchen, but I had to do something. Panic coursed through my veins. What would it take for Sami to let me into her world? I'd gladly give up my own. I didn't want a life without her and Carmen in it.

"When are you leaving for Taiwan?" Sami asked. Her voice was cold, colder than it had been in some time.

I set the pot on the rack, wrung out the dishcloth and dried my hands. "I was supposed to leave on Tuesday."

"Why are you selling your house?"

"Why not?" I asked. Being defensive wouldn't help, but I couldn't stop myself. She'd told Carmen to tell me *goodbye*. "Don't pretend you would ever live there."

"Uh, no."

"Exactly. Someone once said I was using the house to compensate for, what was it? Something about my penis."

"I'm sure I don't know anyone that crude," she said primly.

"Yeah, okay." I scoffed.

She gripped the side of the island. Her eyes blazed. Her hair was up in a tight bun. When had that happened? "Just say it. You're leaving on Tuesday and not coming back."

"I- well, that's a leap of logic, but fine, let's say I am. What of it?" I needed her to give me some sign. I'd get on my knees and worship her for the rest of my life if she would only say that she wanted me to.

"What of it?" Sami echoed. "Because that's what you do, right? You just drift through life from project to project, place to place. You don't change for anyone."

"Give me a reason to stay," I said without looking at her. Instead, I plotted a path to the front door. Sami didn't care, and I was too close to begging. I shouldn't have given up the action film. I'd need something to fill the empty days ahead. Maybe someone would give me a labor intensive job on a crew. I could work on a B unit, something behind the scenes where I could just work and not think.

"I love you," she said.

I started for the door. How many times had Sami told me she hated me? I couldn't deny it any longer. "You know, if you keep saying that, one of these days, I'm going to believe you," I said. That day was today. She hated me. I'd been a fool to think otherwise. *Wait*.

I turned back. Sami's eyes appeared very large, wide, and uncertain.

"You didn't say you hate me," I said.

She shook her head.

"What did you say?"

"I said, I love you."

All the air left my lungs in a rush. "You do?"

She nodded, still hanging back at the island. I walked a few steps toward her. My feet didn't feel like they were actually attached to my body. Everything felt surreal, like the world had tilted on its axis. "Come here," I said.

Sami crashed into my arms. I held her and reached up to free her hair. "Never wear your hair up ever again," I said.

She pulled back enough to look at me. "I give the orders around here, Mister."

I smiled. *That's my girl.* "Then give me some direction, and I'll follow you anywhere."

"Even to Germany?"

"I like Germany. Should I stay home and take care of Carmen while you work?"

She shook her head. "I have a nanny who wants to see Europe."

"Who?"

"Adrianna. I offered her an apartment, and plenty of Eurostar tickets, in addition to her regular pay. She jumped at it."

"And if I come with you?" I asked. *Where do I fit in?* was the real question.

Sami ran her fingers through my hair. I loved it when she did that. "Then you can work as much or as little as you want."

"You make me sound like a kept man," I teased.

Sami laughed. "Then it's decided. We're keeping you."

Chapter Forty-Two

SAMI (SIX MONTHS LATER)

The scent of dinner greeted me when I opened the door to the flat, along with Jarrod's voice singing "*Bei Mit Bist Du Shein.*" He danced swing style with Carmen in the living room. "*Bella, bella,*" Jarrod sang.

"*Wunderbar!*" Carmen shouted, right in time. She spotted me and came running over. "Mommy! We made spaghetti!"

Jarrod followed. He pulled me tight against his chest and kissed me. My heart still pounded every time he did that. "Hello, dear, how was your day?" he asked, his voice low and sultry.

"Better now," I said, and surveyed the sauce-spattered cooktop.

"Still getting used to that sauté pan?" I teased.

"I prefer a wok," he said, donning an apron. "We can sit down in fifteen minutes."

"I set the table," Carmen said.

"I'll go wash up for dinner, then," I said. Carmen grinned and bounced back into the kitchen.

"I better keep an eye on her," Jarrod said.

I grabbed him by his collar and pulled him in for a deeper kiss. "I love that you're all domesticated."

Jarrod grinned. His dark eyes sparkled. "I love you. After the munchkin goes to bed, I'll take off everything but the apron."

The image made me chuckle. "Is that a spatula in your pocket, or are you just happy to see me?" This was us, corny jokes and home cooked meals followed by anime and bedtime stories. I wouldn't have thought it possible that we could be content with such simple things. Adrianna explored the club scene and experienced Europe. Jarrod made sure she had long weekends more often than not. He claimed to get a lot accomplished when Carmen was at preschool or taking a nap. He often worked through the night while I slept so he could work on Los Angeles time. He could sleep in short bursts and wake up refreshed. I wished I could master that habit.

Work still consumed most of my waking hours, but I was better at compartmentalizing now. When I was home, everything disappeared but Carmen and Jarrod. Jarrod did the same when we were all together. He turned his laser focus on the two of us, and we both enjoyed that attention. Carmen called Jarrod "Dad" when she thought I couldn't hear. I wouldn't have objected, but I let her have her secret. We would talk about it when she was ready. She operated on her own schedule, just like she always had.

I was fine with that, except when it came to bedtime. Jarrod stepped in to make the nightly routine more acceptable to my daughter, but she often managed to finagle an extra story or song out of him.

"She gets her stubbornness from you," Jarrod teased as he joined me on the couch after a ten minute story turned into two stories and three songs.

"And I suppose your influence has not contributed a bit to our daughter's headstrong tendencies?"

He stared at me, his face soft with wonder.

"What?"

"You called her ours."

"Am I supposed to pretend she doesn't have you wrapped around her little finger?"

"And what about you? Do you want me wrapped around your finger?" He didn't sound like he was joking. He stroked the top of my ring finger on my left hand.

"You know I only appreciate your Sting impersonations in bed," I said, patting his cheek and running, as usual, from this dangerous topic.

"Okay," he said, not quite sighing.

"Let's talk about it after your next project," I said, not quite looking at him. "Carmen will be starting school. If we can make the schedule work, we'll consider something more... concrete."

He chuckled. "You know how to take the romance right out of the moment, don't you?"

"I just meant..."

He tucked my hair behind my ear. I wore it down now. Jarrod liked it that way. "I waited years just to be with you. If you want to put off the formalities, that's okay. I'll wait as long as you want me to."

We were his, even without the legal document. Surely he knew that. I kissed him, because that spoke louder than words. Jarrod pulled me onto his lap and deepened the kiss. The sound of small feet drew us apart. Carmen stood with her toes on the edge of the rug.

"Aren't you supposed to be in bed?" I asked. I couldn't make my voice sound as stern as it should, not after that conversation. Besides, she looked so cute in her Wonder Woman pajamas, her curls tousled from sleep.

She looked at us, bleary eyed and confused. "I don't remember how the story ended."

I shifted, so I was more on the couch than Jarrod's lap. Carmen saw the space there for her, but hesitated until Jarrod beckoned. She came over and climbed up into her favorite spot, snuggled between the two of us.

"It ended the way all good stories end," Jarrod said. "With 'happily ever after.'" He looked at me as he said it.

I rolled my eyes, but couldn't keep the smile from my lips. This is what I had been reduced to, song lyrics and silly lines from fairy tales. Surprisingly, I was okay with that.

WANT SOME MORE?

For bonus content from the Hollywood Writers and to be the first to hear about new steamy romance from Jael Tempts, sign up for the newsletter!

Find out more at JaelTempts.com

ABOUT THE AUTHOR

Jael Tempts is a crazy cat lady and science fiction nerd who knows that bow ties are cool, browncoats are forever, and the force is with her, always. She and her spouse speak their own language of movie quotes and song lyrics. She is prone to sudden outbursts of showtunes.

ACKNOWLEDGMENTS

Special thanks to my husband, Gene, for reasons too numerous to list.

To my editor, Beth Hale, thanks for everything.

To the SWFL fiction writers' group for feedback and encouragement.

And to the SWFL Romance Writers, I'm so glad to be in a group of fun, supportive writers.